BORDER PIECES

A Morgan Winfeld Novella

By Pam Robertson

Border Pieces
A Morgan Winfeld Novella

By Pam Robertson

ISBN: 978-0-9918569-9-2 (digital version)
978-0-9918569-9-2 (print version)

First Edition

Dedication

This book is for Jill and Peter.
You instilled a love for books in me,
and showed me the joy of wandering
the stacks in search of a good read.
You read to me and have
shared your love –
whether it was good book,
a magazine,
or a piece of poetry,
and you never worried
when I read into the dark hours of the night.
This story couldn't exist
without both of you,
and I wouldn't
be much of a reader.
I love you both so much, and always.

PART 1

CHAPTER 1

Morgan's phone buzzed against her hip. "Leaves are off the trees," the message said. It was code for, "Message received. Cover blown. Expect unorthodox greeting." If the message had said "feet dry," it would have confirmed that he had arrived without detection. Feet dry would have meant their greeting would be polite and cordial, but Jake had seen her text warning him that she had been followed.

She had been well briefed about the agent she was picking up at the Halifax airport, though Morgan had met him two years previously at a conference. She remembered him because he stuck out like a sore thumb among the security professionals and former spies that were there. She was expecting a textbook tall, dark, handsome fellow in his early forties, with well defined features and stunning green eyes. Not that the briefing said his eyes were stunning specifically, but in her memory, they were sure notable. He was just off another assignment and his hair would be cropped short to complement his military uniform, which would make him easy to spot.

Morgan stood back from the crowd around the arrival doors, close to the end of carousel number three. A few moments later she could see passengers coming down the escalator, their legs coming into view first. Among them, a tall soldier in a Canadian camouflage uniform. She knew it was him before she could see his face and the burgundy beret fitted tightly on his head. *So much for subtlety,* she thought.

Jake made a beeline for Morgan the moment he was through the automatic doors. He swept her into a tight hug and nuzzled against her face while whispering, "Sorry about the outfit. Best we could do on short notice. Can I kiss you to make this real?"

Morgan turned her face toward him expectantly, and Jake leaned in to kiss her full on the lips. Not your average 'nice to be home kiss,' rather, this was one of those knee melting, this is Morgan catching her breath kisses. As they drew apart Morgan looked sideways toward a pillar to let Jake know where the two goons were leaning. Jake blinked twice to let her know that he understood.

As they waited for the carousels to move and signal the luggage arrival, Jake sidled up from behind Morgan and put his arms casually around her shoulders. She leaned into him. He nuzzled the back of her hair. "You smell good," he said quietly. Her muscles tensed ever so slightly under her t-shirt.

"You aren't supposed to behave like that in a Canadian uniform," she said quietly.

"Yeah, but they never said that you smelled good. Honestly, I've been thinking about getting close to you since we met at that conference."

"When was the last time you were this close to a woman?" she whispered.

"Ages," he replied, breathing her in. "You smell like sweet citrus."

Morgan turned to face him, her well manicured eyebrows emphasizing her bright blue eyes, and said quietly, "Then listen mister, this is work, so despite you being all cuddly right now, you need to know that this stops the second we get to the car."

"I know," he said, smiling. "I'm just playing it up for the audience, but a bloke can realize a dream, no?" He leaned in with a wink, just as the carousel alarm shrieked and the sounds of luggage being thumped onto the conveyor belt could be heard from behind the wall.

"How subtle is your vehicle?" Jake asked, throwing his duffel bag over one shoulder, as they headed across the airport toward the doors.

"Very," she replied. "Black, North American. Race car engine that I had built especially for me, so it's a sportscar under the hood. Not that great environmentally, but it'll get us out of here in a hell of a hurry."

They moved swiftly through the crowd, watching for the two goons. Her car was parked in the no parking zone directly in front of the airport. Morgan waved thanks to the security guard for watching it. She had paid him a hundred bucks, but it never hurt to be pleasant. Jake threw his duffel into the back.

"Cute plate," Jake said as he shut the trunk and noticed her license plate.

"It works really well out here. I have seven of them in sequence that I can change as needed and people never question them. They look at it for the picture of the cute little birds that we are trying to save, not the series of letters and numbers." Morgan's dedication to conservation causes was important to her, so she had splurged on the Nova Scotia license plates for her car, but she wasn't about to let Jake know all that. The guy could kiss, obviously, and they were assigned to work together, but their mission was all that was important right now. That, and clearing the memory of how well Jake could kiss.

"I am anticipating we'll have to do a little bit of a decoy drive," Morgan said as she started up the car. "If the two guys back there are the same ones that have been tailing me for the last 24 hours, they'll follow in separate cars. One will be a rental jeep, which is a four-cylinder, beige piece of junk, and the other one was driving a cab, so I'm not sure what he has under the hood. Hopefully this construction will slow them down. "

The airport had been under construction for months, and this was height of the winter where people were travelling south to escape the weather. The place was crowded with travellers and vehicles. Since Morgan had avoided the paid parking garage, she was able to quickly pass the construction signs and reach the highway.

She didn't have to work hard to lose the cab. The second car didn't even make it into her rear-view mirror, and she hoped it was stuck in the line up leaving the paid parking area. She left the highway for a secondary road to make sure they weren't being followed.

"You handle this car very well," Jake said, looking over at her.

"I love to drive," she said, smiling for the first time since they'd met. "Fast is my favourite speed."

She could feel Jake looking at her as she drove quickly and capably down the potholed road. From the corner of her eye, she could see him checking out her face, like he was memorizing her, although he had to have seen her recent picture, and he clearly remembered her from the conference.

"You're staring at me," she said curtly.

"Yes, I am," he replied.

"That's making me uncomfortable."

"Sorry," he said, though she didn't think he meant it.

The day was sunny and clear, a nice break to the wind and fine snow mixed with rain that had hung around all week. Morgan pulled over near a bank of rural mailboxes so that anyone passing them would think she was just checking her mail. She opened the trunk, lifted the liner to grab a new magnetic license plate, and quickly traded it with the old one. She walked to the front of the car and removed the Canadian flag that was flapping from her antenna, careful not to tear it as she separated the Velcro underneath. She handed the little flag to Jake when she got in the car, indicating that he could put it into the glove compartment.

"That was quick," he said, "and smart."

"Yeah," she smiled. She had to remind herself not to flirt with him, but the wobbly feeling in her knees was back. "Now hang on and enjoy the view."

They returned to the highway, and soon crossed the bridge toward downtown Halifax. Morgan was sure they weren't being followed and

12

allowed herself to relax a little. Having people tail her this close to home was unsettling.

"Is this your first time visiting Halifax?" she asked.

"Yeah," Jake answered, his tone friendly and warm. "It's only my second time in Canada. The last time was around Ottawa."

"When the American Embassy was being picketed?"

"One of the times, yeah."

She smiled to herself. *He is a likeable person,* she thought.

"So, how long you been in this business?" he asked, looking out the window at the view of the water below the embankment.

"The chauffeur business, or the...um...consulting business?"

"Both," he smiled at her. She watched out of the corner of her eye to see the brackets curve around his mouth. She thought about kissing him again before quickly looking away. His brown eyes and lightly tanned face were easy to take.

Brown eyes? "I remember your eyes as being green," she commented.

"Contact lenses," he said. "Green eyes tend to make people want to stop and talk to me."

"Good point," she said, and went on to offer her official answer about her career. "I joined the army reserves right out of high school. I wanted it to pay for university, which it did. When I finished my degree, I applied to join the federal government as a career counsellor, but got recruited into a different department, and here I am."

She didn't tell him the whole truth, but it was enough for now.

She didn't tell him that she married her pilot husband when they were both nineteen. She avoided talking about the day that she needed to study for an exam and so her husband went flying with a couple of friends in an ultralight plane they shared. She left out the part where a guy on a farm in the area thought the aircraft was there spying on his family drug operation. The felon shot at the plane to "scare them off" he said at the trial. In reality, he fired six rounds of military grade ammunition from a high-powered rifle, and the plane hit the ground in a raging fireball. Anyway, if Jake was briefed properly, he'd already know most of that.

"So that's my story. What's yours?"

"Not as interesting as yours. More than anything right now, I'd like a shower," Jake said.

"Good thing we're here then," she said, pulling into the underground parking lot.

The apartment was beautiful. The balcony faced the Halifax harbour and the place was spacious and bright. There was no clutter anywhere, just how Morgan liked it.

"The main bathroom is first door on the left, off the hall. Your room is straight across the hall," she said waving her arm as a substitute for a guided tour. She headed to the window to check for trouble.

Jake took his duffel to the bedroom and dropped it on the floor before heading into the bathroom, stripping off his shirt as he went.

She heard the shower running and didn't miss a beat when Jake emerged twenty minutes later, relaxed and tanned against a black t-shirt, long legs in black denim, and a pair of well-worn but polished ankle boots.

"I suppose you're hungry," she said.

"Yup, they never feed you on those flights anymore. Whatcha got to eat?" he said, pulling open the door to the stainless-steel fridge. Morgan felt a twinge of embarrassment that there were a few bottles of water, a container of yogurt, two different kinds of pickles, and a carton of eggs. He looked at her, the message about the lack of food written plainly on his face.

"Sorry," she said, shrugging. "I don't cook much, so check the date on the yogurt if you decide to have some."

"When do we leave for Fort McMurray?" he asked.

"Not for another four days."

"Where can we go for a beer and some food?" He took a second look at her. "You've changed your hair or something."

"Yup, I do that a lot when I know bad guys are looking for me. Of course, hiding you is a bit more of a challenge. You're huge." Morgan was a respectable five feet five inches. At 44, she had to work harder to stay in shape than she used to, but she was happy with her fit body. She could walk for hours, and ran nearly every day when she was home. She liked running because she concentrated on every aspect of moving her body and breathing, leaving her no room to ponder other things.

At eight inches taller than Morgan, Jake towered over nearly everyone. They made for an amusing pair as they headed toward the restaurants that bordered the inner harbour.

"So, how'd you end up on this particular assignment?" she asked.

"It was my turn to come to visit Canada once again," he said smiling at her. His smile went right up to his eyes, even with the contacts in them.

"Do you know anything about the oilfields? The industry we're heading into?"

"Not really. Do I need to?"

"Might be useful since we're going to visit the northern parts of it. That and you'll need to be less conspicuous somehow."

"You want me to know what a labourer does? Working in an oilfield job?"

"Something like that," she said, thinking of the massive equipment and the sheer size of the oil sands the last time she visited.

"I can drive all kinds of equipment, and I'm good at covert ops, or blending in as you say. I also have a lot of computer experience, you know, the tampering kind," he said with a wink. "Why are we waiting so long to get out there anyway? Usually I fly in, do the job and get out, same as you."

"Because," she said looking at him, as they walked along the harbour, "this is the new Canada. They aren't crazy about working with our agency, but using a team like ours gives them distance from the outcomes, you know, if we screw something up. We've got to make sure we can go in and do the job without the public figuring out we are there. And, it's better if we come out with turd on our faces than the Canadian's own spy agency or their military. This way the Canadians can't be blamed. They'll help us to accomplish our mission, but they won't admit publicly that any of us are working on something of this nature. Things here have changed a lot in the last few years. The government has become more cautious internationally, and they are fiercely protective of their oil reserves. NAFTA is being re-written under the current American administration, and Canada has re-written their Defense Policy. As a country, they've strengthened ties with the United Kingdom since Britain announced their pull out of the EU. Lately, the relationship with the US has been seriously challenged by tariff announcements and posturing. All of this comes at a huge cost, and the idea is to pay for most of it by harvesting and selling energy. Canada can't afford for things to go wrong in that sector."

Jake tilted his head and encouraged her to continue, which Morgan promptly did. "Canada is a big powerhouse economically, but they fight hard not to be a puppet to the US in issues like trade, even though we are the US' biggest trading partner. It's damned hard – a monumental task to maintain a successful partnership. Plus, there are plenty of problems internally. The criminal element that has evolved here is well organized, has access to money and weapons, and they are very successful at moving around. It may not sound like much, and I know you've just come out of Syria and probably had lots of exposure to bad shit, but terrorists here like to rely on stealth rather than big noise. They are all shades of colour but often Caucasian, they speak English or any of a dozen different languages, including bad guy. They don't look, sound, or seem like terrorists, but they will walk up to you and ask if you have any spare change before very quietly sliding a blade between your ribs. To top all that off, your short hair and upright demeanour make you look like a soldier or a cop. It'd be ideal if we can take that hard edge off you a bit so that you are more relaxed and look like someone who doesn't have a care in the world."

"Right," he said. "I will work on slouching, relaxing, and generally fitting in." His face was closed and serious looking. "So, the agency has been hired by the Canadian government for this job or are we here strictly for the agency?"

"We're here for the agency, but at the request of the Canadian government. They pay money into the agency every year, just as most Commonwealth and a few other countries do, and the urgency of this incident has pushed their requests to the top of our list." Morgan stopped outside a noisy looking place and smiled. "Here it is, the Lower Deck. Great food and beer. Does this look okay to you?" Morgan nodded at the small, tidy looking building with music blaring, and mouth-watering smells making their way out onto the boardwalk.

"Looks good," he said. They lingered over dinner, so they could hear the live band, and enjoy the fresh seafood and locally brewed beer. Their conversation got easier after the first couple of drinks as they remembered their first meeting, and then explored what they had experienced of Canada's borders and politics. Over dessert and coffee, they worked out the details of their fake relationship and cover stories for work. Morgan found the intensity of much of the conversation awkward after the kissing at the airport. She had to remind herself to tend to the job more than once.

CHAPTER 2

Since it was the middle of January, and the height of winter, Morgan wanted to pick up some warm gear before heading to Fort McMurray. The next morning, they stopped at a second-hand store looking for parkas and mitts but didn't find anything suitable for Jake's frame. They left the store and Morgan started searching on her phone as Jake drove her car.

"Crap!" Jake yelled, and slammed on the brakes just short of crashing into a jeep. The jeep driver looked directly at their car and quickly veered off.

Morgan tapped out a number on her phone and spoke into it rapidly. "Stan, yeah it's me. I'm following up on my message earlier. Those guys are way too close to us... no, I am with him now and we just about hit one of them – the jeep. Yes, definitely the same guy that had a friend at the airport yesterday."

"We are very exposed out here," Jake said loudly, his jaw set and the muscle flexing from under his stubbled beard. He was getting familiar with Halifax's streets, but just then they were stopped at a red light. Anyone around them or on the sidewalk had a good view from all sides, as did anyone who might be following them.

Morgan indicated a small alleyway up the block. "Pull into that lane, on your left. Then turn in behind the garbage bins. We can hide for bit." She pulled a styrofoam ball from the glovebox to mask the antenna but had no chance to do anything with it. As soon as they turned into the alley, they came face to face with the damn taxi. It was headed straight for them, and Jake threw the car into reverse. The tires chirped at being forced to change direction so quickly.

"Have you got a gun, perhaps?" Jake asked with an eyebrow lifted.

"A gun?" Morgan laughed. "You're in Canada, Jake. The guns are locked in the safe back at my apartment."

"Shit." He reversed out onto the road and the brakes screeched as he took the corner at speed. A woman on the sidewalk jumped back and pulled two small kids in close. Morgan winced watching as fear crossed the mom's face.

"Just drive, we need to get clear of this neighbourhood," she said.

Jake followed orders. He headed north and then took the ramp onto the freeway. As they sped up, he could see the cab coming up behind them, though the jeep was nowhere in view.

"Take the next exit but ease onto it at the very last second," Morgan said, "then do a quick left at the top, and come down the other side of the highway." Jake maneuvered the car at the last minute, so the cab was unable to make the ramp in time and was forced to keep heading down the highway.

"It'll be a while before he can turn off," she said, "So we've lost him for the time being. Now, where's that jeep?"

"Where do you want me to go?" Jake looked over at her with his brows raised.

Morgan scanned the area around the car, "Looks like we are clear of the two of them, but we still need to find some winter coats," she said. "I have an idea. Let's circle back to the apartment for some overnight gear, and a couple of other things first."

CHAPTER 3

They left the apartment with a backpack each, complete with handguns, ammunition, and knives. Once they reached the highway, Morgan pulled off at a spot overlooking the ocean and turned off the engine. Jake looked at her.

"I want to sweep for bugs. I think maybe we're telling them where we are." She grabbed a gadget from her trunk, and walked slowly around the car. The bug sweeper didn't indicate anything.

"Is the GPS disabled in this jazzed up SUV of yours?" Jake asked as he followed her.

"Yes of course. Fifth rule of spy school is to make sure your own vehicle isn't leaving tracks."

"Has it been serviced lately?" Jake asked carefully.

"Well, yeah it was actually. I was hoping to drive it to Fort McMurray instead of flying, so I had it in last week." She paused as it dawned on her what he had just asked...had the car been outside of her control and possibly been tampered with?

Jake was shaking his head over her comment.

"You wanted to drive to Fort McMurray? In the winter? Isn't that a week's drive from here?" he asked, incredulous.

"Yes, but I don't much like to fly and it wouldn't take us that long if we shared. I like this vehicle. It's a good tool for us."

"In the middle of winter?" He shook his head, and then reached into the vehicle to release the hood.

"I'm choked that I didn't think to look for this earlier," she exclaimed as she and Jake began to look around the vehicle. They both searched under the hood, but there was nothing obvious. Morgan bent to look at the undercarriage, following the exhaust and cables along as she looked for something out of place.

"Found it," she called to Jake, reaching under the carriage and pulling a small transmitter with a bright red light on it. She handed it to Jake for a look.

"No worries," Jake said cheerfully. "Can I throw it in the water, or should I smash it first?"

Morgan was busy looking for a backup unit. "Don't throw it in the water. Some poor lobster might eat the bits. Smash it and toss it in the garbage bin there."

Jake smashed the unit to tiny pieces under the heel of his boot. There wasn't much left to throw into the garbage.

As she drove back to the highway, Morgan had a thought. She passed her phone to Jake and asked him to Google a chain of locally owned used clothing stores that weren't connected to the one they had already visited. She was keen to find some used gear to help with their cover.

The official plan, as designed by Stan, the agency's efficient and technically savvy operations officer, was to look like a newly married middle-aged couple, instead of being seen as spies on the lookout for terrorist activity in the oilsands.

"Did you say this place was called Frenchy's?"

"Yes. If the Frenchy's Used Clothing Store has some gear it'll make it easier for us to look legit, rather than walking into Fort Mac with stuff that is brand new and shiny looking. Besides, we still have a few days to kill and those goons to deal with."

"Well, we could buy new stuff and bash it up a bit to make it look a little worn," Jake offered.

They couldn't find anything at Frenchy's to fit Jake, and headed to Murphy Gear instead. There they found tall sizes, including parkas that were rated to minus 40 degrees Celsius. They added toques, mitts, and heavy boots to the pile.

"Where you going?" asked the curious store clerk, decked out in her own Murphy Gear hoodie and sweat pants.

"On our honeymoon," Morgan said, switching to a stage whisper. "It's a bit of a let down, to be honest. I think I'm about to freeze my ass off looking for polar bears."

The clerk laughed, registering the height difference between the two visitors, but not missing how fit they were.

Jake loaded their gear into the car. "Is there somewhere we can stay nearby? Do we need to get some food first?"

"I know just the place. It's not far and it's secluded. Two more stops – the electronics store and then some groceries, and then we're ready to head there."

Once they were stocked up, Morgan provided directions and Jake drove them to an area on Nova Scotia's western shore. Morgan called Stan on the way to alert him that her downtown apartment was probably compromised because of the tracking device. Once Stan had those details, she asked him to set up a reservation at Spray Harbour, a holiday resort in the area. She asked him to make sure they got a cabin near the water.

The cabins weren't normally open this time of year, so she mentioned to Stan that it was important. This way, if the goons did show up, she and Jake would see them coming, and it was far less likely that civilians would get hurt. The agency liked to keep a low profile, and casualties didn't help with keeping things quiet.

"I'm going to miss that apartment if things get messed up here," Morgan said wistfully. "I really like the view."

"You can always come hide in Ireland for a while after this job," Jake offered. "It's pretty easy to hide there. I do it all the time."

"You'd have to teach me an Irish accent, so I blend in."

"No problem. I'm pretty good with accents."

"So I noticed. You sound pretty Canadian right now."

CHAPTER 4

"Right, cameras are installed as best they could be," Jake said. "Let's do one last walk around the property and make sure we haven't missed anything."

It was still light out, and they took advantage of the time to look for vantage points outside. There were 13 cabins in a row close to the shore, though they weren't normally rented this time of year, due to proximity to the water and freezing cold. Stan had worked some charm so that Morgan and Jake were staying in the first cabin in the row. The other cabins were empty.

There was no sandy beach here, and the grass along the edge of the water had traces of snow and frost. They stood for a moment listening as the ocean lapped rhythmically at the icy rocks.

Back at the cabin, Morgan said, "I'm going to check out the shower." She headed up the polished wooden staircase two steps at a time.

"We're at a bit of a disadvantage here," Jake said when Morgan returned damp and smelling of citrus again. "The wi-fi signal isn't steady, and I keep losing the feed for the cameras. Gad, you smell good."

"We are a bit remote," Morgan offered, ignoring his flirting. "Let's see what we can rig up...or maybe there's no need." She pointed at the jagged image on the laptop.

"Company's coming." Jake said, peering at the screen. "Do we know who this guy is?"

She bent closer to the screen. "He doesn't look like either of the goons. He isn't soft enough. He's big though, and determined looking."

The image on screen was clear, though interrupted with horizontal lines like the start of an old Alfred Hitchcock movie. The man strode purposefully along the gravel road between the main hotel and the cabins. His western style overcoat was doing a good job hiding a rifle if you didn't know better, but Jake and Morgan knew from the hand in his pocket that the assassin was steadying a weapon as he walked on the uneven snow and gravel toward them.

"I think I'd rather meet this guy outside," Jake said reaching for his jacket and sliding into it. "I'll head closer to the water, if you head around to the back of the cabin for cover."

Morgan nodded. There was no need for more conversation. They both knew what needed to be done. She was grateful for her boots in getting over the thin layer of ice and snow that was in the shade of the cabin. She attached the silencer onto her handgun as she moved, and stuck to the shadows.

The assassin wasn't sneaking at all. He was headed right toward the row of cabins as if he belonged there. Jake adopted an equally bold approach as he stepped off the porch.

"Hey mate, don't s'pose you've got a light? Me and the missus want to light a fire," he said in a perfect Australian accent.

Morgan saw the assassin raise a medium length rifle under his coat, preparing to shoot from the hip to take Jake down.

"Hey, don't be an asshole," she heard from Jake, and then a thump as Jake's throwing knife connected with the assassin's shoulder.

Morgan darted from behind the cabin and caught site of the assassin lunging at Jake. Jake stepped aside, then stuck out one foot to trip the other man, who went down with a thump that shook the ground. They rolled into the snow, and Jake was quickly astride the man, who struggled and kicked from below. They fought, grunted, and blood squirted from the shoulder wound, but the knife stayed in place. Jake pounded the assassin in the chin with a right hook and then his left hand quickly removed the knife from the injured shoulder. The assassin flailed his legs and reached up for Jake's face with his good arm. Morgan reached the fray as these two men of equal size and strength worked to kill one another.

She edged toward the fight and shoved her booted foot over the wet bloody patch that was showing on the assassin's coat. She leaned on the wound, and the man's face contorted. She levelled her pistol at him just as Jake delivered another hefty blow to the assassin's face.

Morgan moved her foot, motioning Jake to stay put straddling the now unconscious man. She pulled back his coat to look at the shoulder wound. "He's still bleeding pretty good, but he's breathing. Let's haul him inside."

They picked him up awkwardly due to their difference in height, and dragged the bleeding man into the cabin. By the time they got the door shut it was fully dark outside. There were no sirens or alarm bells, and it seemed that no one at the hotel had reported seeing anything. Jake peered quickly at the dim feed he had for the hotel lobby, but the hotel clerk was nowhere to be seen. He picked up the phone to tell the young girl to call the police, but hung up when the hotel voicemail picked up.

Morgan had pulled the assassin's ID from his back pants pocket. No real assassin carried identification, and this was obviously fake. The ID was for Richard Strauss, and had a picture of their assassin, but everything in the wallet was new and unwrinkled. Morgan sent pictures of it all off to Stan.

"His clothes are not from around here. That coat is something worn by cowboys, on a ranch. See how it opens in the back."

"You mean if he was local he'd have had a different jacket?"

"More likely a parka this time of year," she said.

Jake ripped open the man's shirt. There were no obvious tattoos or scars. Strauss groaned as Jake rolled him over, and secured his wrists with a ziptie. Jake pulled the man's phone from another pocket and grunted as he took note of the password protected screen.

It didn't take long for Jake to prove what kind of "tampering" skills he had as he popped the SIM card out from the phone and clicked it into a reader on his laptop. There was no personal information or a contact list but there were encrypted conversations that he started to run through an analyser.

"Is it possible this guy is alone, d'ya think? Where are the other goons that have been following us?" Jake said, spreading his hands out to the air. He looked as perplexed as Morgan felt. She noticed that his cheeks were flushed from the fight, and he looked sexy as hell.

The man stirred, and Jake propped him up on a kitchen chair. Morgan handed Jake a folded tea towel to apply to the wound, although he was not bleeding much now. Strauss didn't say anything, just looked at them both from under furrowed eyebrows and kept his mouth shut.

"I don't know," Morgan replied, thoughtful. "If the goons were with him they should have crashed the party by now."

"Are you here alone?" Jake asked Strauss. "You wouldn't have come here alone, or you'd be an idiot. Where are your friends?" Jake demanded, bending down to look the man in the eyes.

Strauss didn't reply. He clamped his lips together, blood around his mouth forming into a morbid grimace.

"We'd best just leave him tied up here and get moving," Morgan said gathering her things. "Strauss if you don't want to talk, fine, but we're leaving you here so either tell us who to call, or hope your friends know how to find you." She ripped the cord from the landline out of the wall as Jake gathered their camera gear.

"Last chance," Jake said. "Anyone you'd like us to call?"

"Go fuck yerselves," Strauss said, blood and spittle easing their way down his chin.

"Suit yourself," Morgan said coolly.

Morgan and Jake stopped at the hotel desk to advise the clerk of the package in their cabin. They found her body behind the desk, her young neck broken.

"Clearly this assassin either had more skill than he showed today, or he had helpers somewhere," Morgan said quietly to Jake. They looked briefly around the lobby but saw nothing else out of order.

Morgan's hair on her arms suddenly stood up, and she was sure they weren't alone. She looked at Jake and tipped her head toward the door behind the reception desk, indicating to Jake she was going to open it. He raised his pistol and nodded to Morgan, ready to back her up.

Morgan approached the side of the reception desk, when the door behind the dead girl burst open, and there they were. Goons one and two, with pistols drawn and pointed. One of the men – the heavier of the two whom Morgan recognized as the jeep driver, raised his pistol to shoot, and just as quickly went down onto the floor as he tripped over the dead girl. Goon two, in his taxi driver's jacket, was more surefooted, and managed to squeeze off a round just as Morgan's bullet caught him in the middle of his pronounced forehead.

"Nice shot. I will try and remember not to piss you off," Jake whispered as he bound the hands of the jeep driver.

Morgan looked around the reception area, searching for more trouble, but the place was deserted. She pulled out her phone, and used the voice command to call Stan. He answered on the third ring, sounding like he had been asleep, which was to be expected since he was in London, England.

"Okay, Morgan, I'm on it." Stan said, his voice quickly losing it's fatigue and replaced with directness and assurance. "You'll be on the next flight to Edmonton. Is it safe for you to go to the Halifax airport, or do you need to go somewhere else? The jet is in Halifax but I can have it meet you anywhere."

"There's not a whole lot of options, Stan. We're heading to the airport."

A text arrived to Morgan's phone as they reached the airport, and Jake read it to Morgan. Their private flight would take them from Halifax to Edmonton, and finally on to Fort Mac, as the locals called it.

The next text covered off the issue of supplies. "At your Edmonton stop, we will load two secure bins onto the plane with everything you need. Enjoy your flight."

CHAPTER 5

Ten hours later, and adjusting to a three hour time change, Morgan and Jake finally landed in Fort McMurray. There were heaps of snow plowed to the edges of the airport, and the roadways throughout the city were framed in windrows. Their breath came out in clouds in front of them and Morgan could feel frost sticking to her eyelashes as they waited for the attendant to bring their rental car. It was cold here, even by northern Alberta standards for January.

When they got to the hotel, Jake wrangled a luggage cart to the car, so they could easily move their weapon stash without taking extra trips. They wrestled the inadequate frame back across the parking lot, entered the hotel, and stomped snow off their boots.

"Evenin'," smiled the clerk, chipper from her warm position behind the counter. "Reservations?"

Jake did a tour around the lobby and surrounding hallway as Morgan checked them in. It was a typical cheap hotel created for a high turnover of guests, and it was not a place that was particularly safe for people in the business of covert operations. There were outside exits that could be propped open, thin walls, and although there was a security camera in the lobby, there was no red light indicating that it was working. He'd seen worse, but it was disturbing after what had happened in Nova Scotia.

He looked at Morgan with raised eyebrows, and she read his message clearly. This place was going to be like staying in a matchbox.

CHAPTER 6

Morgan was speaking with Stan and working on coordinates when a knock on the door got Jake quickly to his feet. The restaurant connected to their hotel had sent a selection of grub, including hot chicken wings, fries, deep fried pickles, and a thermos of decaf coffee.

"There's no beer here," Jake said looking at the pile of food, disappointment in his voice.

"Sorry, I didn't think we should drink since we're on duty. Besides it's damned cold out and that's more like coffee weather than beer." Morgan put some humour in her voice, "Did you notice there's only one bed in here? That's awkward."

"It's okay, I can take the couch for the first night."

"First night? You sleep on the couch tonight and you're on it the entire time we are here. I don't think it even pulls out into a bed."

"S'okay, I don't think I'd fit on it as a pull out anyway," he said, eyeing up the firm looking sofa. It was a typical cheap hotel piece of furniture. A mustard colour when it was new, now faded to a dirty shade. The fabric was taut over the stuffing, and although it appeared to be clean, it wasn't very inviting looking.

"You might have made the better choice, actually," Morgan said as she sat on the edge of the bed and gave it a bit of a bounce. "This thing feels like a carboard box."

Morgan thought about their kisses at the airport. She watched his long legs take three quick steps to close the gap as he moved across the room to sit on the couch. Every time she allowed herself an unguarded moment she had a physical response to whatever he was doing. Just now, even his stubbled chin looked delicious.

He patted the couch beside him. "Come sit here," he smiled. "I'll not bite you."

They shared their pub food, and wiped greasy fingers on napkins that dissolved into nothing. "Those are shite," Jake declared, shaking napkin shreds from his hand.

"Those pickles were good, though," Morgan said, not even trying to suppress a burp.

Jake laughed. "I'm glad we are through the awkwardness of not burping in front of each other."

"Just like an old married couple," Morgan smiled. She looked at him closely. He'd taken his contacts out and his eyes were a bright beautiful green staring back at her.

"Don't tease," he said, "Or I may just kiss you like an old married man."

"Oh, I happen to have it on good authority that you don't kiss like that at all."

Jake looked at her, and then turned to face her on the couch. "Are we working and being professional right now, or are we working on our guise as two 40-somethings who are newlyweds?" he asked, his voice deep and serious.

"We're professionals working out how to share a room together," Morgan said, trying to lighten the mood. "And I'm working on looking at your green eyes without you feeling like I'm staring at you." She paused. "No wonder you like the contacts so people aren't ogling you. You're hard to look away from."

"C'mere," he said softly, drawing her in. "You can look at 'em all you like."

She leaned in toward him, wanting to kiss him, but thinking about the job. His lips brushed hers, and her body flushed hot as he touched her. She leaned in and kissed him back, and felt herself sinking into the scratchy fabric of the couch. She put her hands on his chest and pushed herself away.

"My god you're a great kisser, Jake. But we've got a serious job to do and we don't need chemistry getting in the way."

"You're right," he said regretfully. "Though at least we know we can pull off the newlywed bit." He paused. "I'm going to go down to the bar and grab a beer. Do you want one?"

"Scotch," she said, her voice deep.

CHAPTER 7

"You here working for the cops?" the slightly drunken man at the bar asked Jake. The lounge stunk of spilled beer and stale pizza.

"You look like a cop," the guy said.

"Hell no," Jake replied, offering the stranger a beer. "I'm here with my wife. She's doing some work with an oil company while I get to enjoy some time off."

"Days off are pretty uncommon around here. You either get fired or suspended if you want time off. Or y'end up dead."

"Dead?"

"Never mind," the man's face closed, and the light left his eyes as he took the last drink of his beer.

"Well, I just wrapped up ten years with a computer company and got canned," Jake said the lie easily. "So, I'm due for some time off. What do you do?"

"I operate heavy equipment on a site near here. And send a lotta alimony home to the ex. Can you operate a forklift? Maybe a bobcat?"

"I can, but I'm more of a desk jockey type. Computers, technology. That kind of stuff."

"Well, if ya want a job at the site, I can getcha an intro," he offered in a friendly tone.

"That'd be great."

When Jake returned to the hotel room, Morgan had a computer set up and was looking at screen. "I'm just organizing files so when I get to the Human Resources office tomorrow, I look like I know what I'm doing. How were things at the bar?"

"I have a sort of job interview set up, so it's looking good," he said, placing a glass beside her on the desk.

"Ha ha, someone offered you an introduction?" She picked up the glass and smelled it, expecting a mix of peat and earth.

"Yeah, exactly. Why?"

"If they refer someone for a job and the new person passes their probationary period, the person that introduces them earns a cash bonus. That guy's smart. What's in this glass?"

"The bartender swears it's Scotch, but I saw him pour it from a bottle that said Crown Royal."

Morgan closed one eye to stop the fumes from making it water, her and took a tiny sip. "My Grandpa used to drink that, but he always added water and ice," she said.

"Yeah, it smells a bit like a hardass drink. Anyway, the guy at the bar mentioned that people here don't leave. They either get fired, suspended, or end up dead. What do you suppose he meant by that?"

For months, the buzz about security threats had been increasing steadily in the area. Initially it looked like a drug related thing, and there was no mistake that drugs were a big problem in the region. The big oil companies had dry camps and contracts with their employees that there were no alcohol or drugs allowed on site. The staff in safety sensitive positions – from equipment operations, to welding, and even cooking, could be tested at any time. If staff were found to be using, the company might send them for detox or counselling, but if the employee didn't comply, or couldn't stay clean, they got fired.

In addition to oil industry employees, there were thousands of people working support roles in Fort McMurray and the surrounding area. They worked in hotels, restaurants, grocery stores, lounges, and every possible hospitality and service job they could. The pay was poor in those support roles, so it wasn't unusual to see young workers living in crowded apartments, sharing everything from their beds to clothing. Drugs were a common component of communal living.

As they reviewed their briefing notes, Morgan and Jake focussed on work. The RCMP, Canada's national police force, had a detachment in the area, and had spent the last nine months gathering intelligence on what looked like a new gang smuggling drugs into Fort McMurray. Police had made some arrests, but the suspects were so low on the chain that they apparently didn't know who they were selling the stuff for.

As police uncovered problems and worked with the security teams connected to the oil companies, more threats were uncovered. The local police brought in help from Calgary, Edmonton, and Toronto. Another arrest at Fort MacKay, 50 kms away, had resulted in a police seizure of hundreds of pills, cocaine, brass knuckles, marijuana, a high powered unsecured rifle, additional drug paraphernalia, and a stack of money.

Just this month police had made another drug bust, this time directly in Fort McMurray. Drugs, including powerful and highly dangerous fentanyl were present, along with small amounts of heroin, cocaine, marijuana, and meth. The owner of the house had next to nothing in his bank account, and although there was a jean jacket found in the garage with patches identifying a drug gang, there were no other signs.

Morgan turned her head at the sound of a local TV news story. "Egads," she said. "Alicia Stars is coming up here to protest the oil sands. Why does she need to do that just now?"

"Protest?" said Jake. He hadn't heard of the bevvy of stars and celebs that liked to fly over the oil sands and declare the place unfit for humanity, all the while raising their own celebrity. "Jeez, what a waste of time. Who pays the celebs for these trips?"

Morgan let out a long slow breath, "I think we are about to find out."

CHAPTER 8

The best way to get answers about some things was to hit the internet and do some creeping around on social media, Morgan knew. She called Stan, so he could reach out to some of his sources and do some online intel gathering. There were people at the agency referred to as friendly hackers, or grey hackers, because they could track down all kinds of information and they had access to some very good digital kit. It didn't take them long to determine who was funding Stars' trip, and to see who was behind a few other high rollers over the years.

"On the surface," Stan said over their secure line, "it looks like some anti-government, environmental type group is paying for these trips, and giving your celebs huge fees. But with some digging around, it looks like the sources are anti-establishment folks, drug gangs, and they may be Canadian, but they are working with people from the mid-western states."

"I don't want to know how you figure these things out, do I, Stan?" Morgan said as she rubbed her temple with her free hand.

"It's all done through algorithms and then some real digging, Morgan. We look at who is following their social media accounts, and then trace back to see when there has been a spike in followers and interactions, and boom. Within 9-12 months that star is off on some high profile rant, paid for with suspicious money. We're looking deeper at it right now."

"So, these guys play nice with Stars, and get hold of her publicist and stuff to get her hired to do a high profile campaign? Then what?"

"Then they use the sensationalism and attention as a diversion to get what they really want, which is hacking computers, accessing security, and blowing things up or making people think they are going to blow something up."

"So, what are we looking at here," Jake interjected. "Some kind of ruse for a security hack? Blowing up stuff? Drugs? Or more?"

"That's what you guys are there to find out. Without getting caught, of course. It seems like there is some kind of link to the fire you'll be investigating.

Morgan disconnected the call and looked at Jake.

"Kissing was a lot more fun than contemplating someone blowing up this place, hey?" he teased.

Morgan threw the cell phone at him but instead of it hitting him in the head, he caught it in his long fingers and set it down while he grinned at her.

CHAPTER 9

Morgan poured over the disjointed pieces of intel they had so far. They needed to get a better idea of whether the drug busts were somehow linked to a security threat, the fire of 2016, or they were a red herring. The local police were a division of the Royal Canadian Mounted Police, the RCMP. Morgan called the office for the commander of the RCMP detachment for Wood Buffalo, the region including Fort McMurray and the surrounding area, and booked an appointment for the following day.

Flicking through an email from Stan, Morgan read a briefing note about Commander Marcus Sheridan. He had been at the Wood Buffalo RCMP detachment for 5 years. He was involved in the community, coaching kid's hockey, singing tenor in the church choir, and he was an avid outdoorsman. The proudest moment of his RCMP career was to be promoted to the position of detachment commander and posted to the community where he'd been born, and where he had spent his childhood. He'd been married to Maeve for 35 years. They had two grown sons, aged 30 and 34, both married, with five grandchildren between them.

Early the next morning, Morgan and Jake arrived at the RCMP detachment. They stopped in at the reception window and checked in with the duty officer, who hailed her boss on a speaker phone. The detachment wasn't very big, and they could hear the loudspeaker from where they waited.

"I could just go back there and knock on the door," offered Jake helpfully after they didn't receive a response.

The duty officer didn't smile. She nodded curtly, her tight bun bouncing as she clipped, "If you did that, I'd have to shoot you." If she hadn't winked at Jake as she delivered the statement, Morgan would have believed she was serious. It seemed as though Jake had all kinds of luck with women whether his eyes were green or not.

Morgan leaned in to interrupt their flirting. "He didn't answer you," she said. "Are you sure he's there? He should be expecting us."

"Yes, I saw him go in first thing this morning. Follow me, and I'll go knock." She rose from her chair and smoothed her uniform pants. *This must be her first posting,* Morgan thought. The young woman was in her early 20s, trim, and serious about her job. She didn't have a noticeable thread of grey in her jet black hair, nor a single line creasing her perfect skin. She knocked on an office door, and opened it, "Boss, you're holding these people up," she said, and then she let out a tiny sound that reminded Morgan of a cat having all the air pushed out of its lungs.

Jake eased the young woman away from the door, so he could get a look inside. "How do we get an ambulance in this place?" he said.

CHAPTER 10

"This was his last posting," Maeve said. Her hands shook as she twisted a tissue. She looked at Morgan. "He was going to retire from here and build a cottage near a lake somewhere closer to our grandkids. What happened? Who would do this to him...to my family?"

Morgan didn't know what to say. She could only watch as Maeve unravelled into small pieces following the short church service. It would be another week before Sheridan's body was flown to Edmonton for a massive RCMP funeral.

"I have to get out of here," Morgan whispered to Jake as people milled around quietly, searching for lukewarm cups of coffee and conversation.

"But everyone in town is here," he said. "This is a helpful place for us to be."

"I...I just need some fresh air."

"Do you want me to come with you?"

"No. It's fine."

She left the reception area quickly, her breath coming in small gasps as she pawed the coatracks looking for her parka. *All those people meant well toward Maeve,* she thought. The hugging. The words of comfort. But she knew, Morgan did, that those comforts just went so far and then there was nothing. The visits from those same friends and family would come to a stop after a few weeks. The phone would stop ringing. The gap would widen and grow ugly because it was followed by Maeve's gradual realization that there were no texts or calls from her husband asking if he should stop for milk on his way home. There would be no more surprise bottles of wine and pizza for supper, or anything at all. The memories of Morgan's own loss flooded every part of her body.

The cold air hit her sharply as she exited the church, and brought her back to the present.

"Stop being such an idiot and get your shit together, Morgan!" she told herself harshly. She fought with her zipper because the bottom of the damned thing on her very warm parka was slightly out of reach of her arms. "This is what a fuckin' Tyrannosaurus rex must've felt like," she sighed.

Out of the corner of her eye, she caught movement on the street that ran alongside the church. Someone had just laid down in their car to avoid her glance, she was sure of it. She scurried up the icy windrow to make it look like she was preparing to cross the road, and tried to get a better look at the car. She could see a white sedan, and the exhaust coming up out of the rear end. The car looked new and clean, and it stood out like a sore thumb among the big pick up trucks and SUVs. *It has to be a rental,* Morgan thought. Someone from out of town maybe here for the memorial, but if that was the case, why were they out in the frigid parking lot and not inside at the reception?

Morgan climbed down the other side of the windrow, and headed for the walkway on the opposite side of the street. She wished fleetingly that they hadn't chosen to walk from the hotel to avoid taking up parking space at the memorial.

She hesitated for a moment, wondering if she should go back and get Jake, then told herself to stop being emotional. As far as anyone in this city new, she was a career counsellor brought in to do some work at one of the oil sites. She was not on the verge of a panic attack from thinking about her dead husband. Everyone here thought Jake was her husband, not her partner on a case. No one in that car was watching her. It was probably just someone who had climbed in their car to stay out of the cold while they grabbed a smoke.

But then again, if they were just out for a smoke, why duck out of the way? Her practical nature kicked in and she realized that in a car, the person could be doing any number of things they did not want seen. Smoking pot, taking a hit of something else, or even taking a nap could all be reasons to move out of sight.

As she made her way down the sidewalk, the wind pushed her forward and tried to work its way into the fabric of her parka. Morgan heard the car clunk as the transmission was put into gear, then heard snow crunch underneath the cold tires. She picked up her pace, and wished that her handgun was in her pocket instead of being tucked into the back of her pants and under a light jacket, totally out of reach under the bulk of her damned parka. She heard running from behind her and whipped her body around, only to see Jake approaching. The car accelerated and moved off.

"Any idea who that was?" Jake asked through the high collar of his coat.

"No, but he gave me the heebie jeebies."

"He certainly seemed to be watching you as I left the church. That's why I ran to catch up with you."

They walked along in silence, with the sound of crunching snow echoing through their bodies in the cold.

Morgan texted Stan to let him know she would call with an update shortly, while Jake surveyed the neighbourhood. As they entered the hotel parking lot, Morgan nudged Jake. "That's the car from the church," she said.

They entered the hotel just as Magrath, who had been driving the white car, left the foyer for his room. Jake bent quickly in front of the counter as if to pick something up. He looked at the clerk, who was prepared to give him anything that he wanted despite being 20 years his junior.

"That guy just dropped this. I'll take it to him. What room is he going to?"

"214," the girl said, and then she caught herself, "...but I shouldn't have told you that."

"Don't worry," said Jake. "I won't tell him." He winked at her and the girl blushed.

CHAPTER 11

"Let's not allow him to get comfortable," Morgan said when they got to their own room. "Or for that silly girl to tell him you have something."

"Agreed. Grab your stuff, and let's go pay him a visit."

They exited their room carefully, with guns and silencers tucked in at their backs, and each with a small knife in their boot. No one was about as they crept quietly up the stairs to the second floor.

From their vantage point at the door to the stairwell, Jake could see the door to Room 214 being held open with the latch. The occupant wouldn't be far. He eased himself back into the stairwell and updated Morgan with two words. "Door's open," he whispered. He slipped his revolver from his back, and Morgan did the same with hers.

A few moments later, Jake heard someone walking down the hallway. He peeked out the stairwell door. There was a man approaching with an ice bucket in one hand and two bottles of pop tucked into his elbow. Two bottles meant he was probably not traveling alone. Jake turned to Morgan and held up two fingers, so she knew the man wasn't alone.

This hotel had installed hydraulic arms on the individual hotel doors so that the doors shut quietly but effectively when a guest entered their room. Once the man was through his door and it began closing slowly behind him, Jake slipped from the stairwell in a move that was part jaguar and part ape, Morgan thought. He quietly placed his foot at the bottom of the door, pushed hard, took a step into the room, and thrust the door into the back of the unsuspecting man. The plastic pop bottles Magrath had in his arms hardly landed and the ice was still rolling on the carpet as Morgan entered behind Jake.

She made sure the door closed tight, took in her surroundings, and locked eyes with a woman seated on the edge of the bed. The woman shook herself, and reached across to the nightstand where a 4-inch serrated knife lay open. She stopped moving just short of the knife as a bullet from Morgan's gun hit her in the temple. Blood quickly spread over the crisp white hotel bedspread.

Morgan turned slightly in the small room to give Jake room as he wrestled with the man. Jake was so large that it wasn't much of a struggle to keep himself across the smaller man's back.

"Magrath, you worm! Why are you here?"

"To kill you Jake, of course! Fulfilling a dream."

"You've tried to kill me before and failed. Today won't be any different," Jake said through gritted teeth. His Irish accent was unmistakeable. He picked up Magrath's head and bashed it into the carpet.

"Who sent ye?" Jake said through gritted teeth.

"Not telling you, bastard," Magrath said through his bloodied mouth.

Morgan could see that Jake had a good grip on whomever he was sitting on. She started searching belongings in the room to see what was there. Nothing but menus and directions to turn on the TV, until she got to the woman's small handbag. In the bottom, below the lining, were two passports, credit cards, and some cash.

"Dalgliesh," she read off the passports. "Wasn't he a British TV cop or something?"

Magrath – or Dalgliesh – continued to struggle, but he wasn't getting very far. Jake leaned in close and hissed at him. "So you're an Irishman pretending to be a British TV cop, eh Magrath? How the mighty have fallen." He delivered a blow to the side Magrath's head, stunning the smaller man. Jake bound Magrath's hands tightly behind his back with a plastic tie, then roughly picked the unsteady man up by the shoulders and dumped him in the room's only chair.

"What's the deal Magrath? What the hell are you doing here? You're a long way from home."

Magrath squinted one eye shut, his greasy hair hanging across his forehead and the blood from a very crooked nose and split lip spraying as he spoke. "You bastard, Jake. You're why I am here. Yer dealin' with people who have lots of money and don't care what it takes to shut you up."

"So, are you here because of something I am working on right now, or something from the past Magrath?"

"You killed my partner, and your best friend, and I was always going to kill you, but you know I don't do nuthin' for free." Magrath sprang from the chair, aiming his head at Jake's midsection, but Jake was much faster.

"Magrath, you stupid bastard. You know there is no turning back now," Jake said, catching the hurtling man. Morgan was ready with her pistol but there was no need. Jake held his knee up and caught the man in the face. Magrath dropped to the floor again, not moving this time.

Morgan sighed. There was no big Hollywood scene with people crashing through thin walls, or someone calling the cops because of thuds and bangs from room 214. There had been one shot fired with a silencer, and a little scuffle, and that was it. The Dalgliesh's were checked out.

"How the hell did he find us here, after all this travel and secret identities, contact lenses, and hair changes?" Morgan thought out loud as she took a long sip of Crown Royal back in their room.

"Damned if I know," Jake said looking at his hand and flexing his fingers. "I think this middle knuckle is out of place a bit. It hurts like a sonofabitch."

"Oh here, let me see it, you big baby. I know how to do this."

He offered his hand with no hesitation. Morgan looked at his long fingers, and stroked the joints gently, the heat from her hands penetrating his roughened skin. "Do you want a drink of anything first? This could hurt."

"I'm a trained killer," he laughed. "It won't hurt much."

"Okay," she said, "consider yourself warned. Sit on the edge of the bed." She stood in front of him. He looked evenly at her, his green eyes glittering. She rubbed her thumb across the joint, getting a feel for it, and then pulled and twisted rapidly on his fourth finger.

"Jesus H. Christ!" came out through his gritted teeth as he tucked his hand into his armpit.

"Don't heat it up, you need to ice it for five minutes on and five off, so it doesn't swell, and so the ice doesn't freeze the tissue."

"You're some kind of ice queen, you know that?" he said with hand tucked between his knees now. He exhaled slowly. "Feck, that hurts!"

She smiled innocently and took another sip from her drink. "Did you know that when you meet other Irishmen your accent comes back?"

"Yeah," he said through gritted teeth. "It's only a problem if there are survivors, so I don't let it worry me much."

Morgan got serious again. "Who was that guy? How did you know him?"

"A long time ago we were part of a teen youth group together, in Ireland. Magrath went north to join the police force, and I went south and joined the military where I trained as a sniper. I'll concede that being a big bloke gave me advantages as a sniper. Makes it tricky being on stakeouts sometimes, but it's super helpful for running and leaping into and out of danger." His smile was back, the pain subsiding.

"And the friend and partner that he mentioned?"

"That was Freddy Keegan. Freddy was a part of our group, but he turned out to be a bad guy, as you would call him. I had to shoot him a couple of years ago though I didn't kill him directly. He was a big time drug runner, and we caught up with him on a smuggling bust in Cork. I intentionally shot him in the arm to just scare him, you know, and stop him from shooting back. He ran off in the dark, into the dockyards, and ended up getting shot a second time, in the head. I think that last shot was from Magrath, but we will never know for sure."

"Oh...I'm sorry you had to shoot an old friend Jake."

"He was only a friend when we were teens, Morgan. As an adult, he was only friends with criminals, and he was no friend of mine, or of Ireland."

"Do you think this means there is a bigger drug issue going on here than we may have thought?"

"If Magrath's involved, maybe, but last I knew he was still a cop in Northern Ireland. If he's got himself mixed up in international work, then I daresay he had moved on. I'll check with Stan."

CHAPTER 12

The next morning dawned bright, sunny, and very cold. Jake and Morgan rose early, and he drove their rented SUV to Walterwell Site. They ate breakfast at the company cafeteria, but didn't talk much as both of them got lost in thought about what they had to do.

Morgan was well prepared for her fake human resources job. She headed down a long hallway and into human resources to see the Vice President of People, or VPOP. *What a pretentious fricking job title,* Morgan thought as she entered the office.

Morgan's cover was to provide career counselling to several injured workers while she poked about the place. Patricia, as VPOP, would join the meetings too, so that they could set up return to work plans that met the needs of the worker and were good for the company. Jake's job was to gather as much intel as he could while Morgan was busy. As it turned out, Morgan wasn't going to be able to get as busy as she had hoped.

"I'm sorry Patricia isn't here to conduct these meetings with you, and I can't even be helpful because I can't access her calendar. Can you handle the interviews on your own?" asked the administrative assistant for the unit. Alix was young, pretty, and eager to help.

"Sure thing, I can do a preliminary meeting with anyone that shows up. It'll help if you can give me access to the electronic personnel records, so I can see what's been done so far."

"Hmm, I don't think there's much entered electronically to be honest. Patricia was working on it, but there wasn't much finished. Let me check for files on her desk."

"Sure, and meanwhile I'll wait and see who arrives for their appointments." Morgan sighed inwardly. Having the VPOP away was going to make for a long, slow day.

The first person in to see her was Jack Frederick. Jack was a welder in his late 30s who had joined the company right out of high school as an apprentice. He was a senior team leader, and one day ended up trapped under a piece of metal shelving that collapsed. He'd nearly lost his left arm, and the scarring was jagged and bumpy where he was missing a chunk of muscle. Morgan led him through some small talk and they talked about Jack's desire to get back to work before Morgan asked him what the company could do to make things better.

"Well, my accident was a fluke," Jack said. "Couldn't have seen that coming, and the company has been real good about making sure I was looked after. They flew me to Edmonton in a small plane, not even waiting for a medevac. I have no complaints at all."

"Okay, that's good to hear, Jack. Anything else you need as you come back to work? We usually start with things like part-time hours, extra physiotherapy to help keep your muscles and joints limber. Anything you can add to that?"

"No ma'am. I like my job, a lot. Although, if you are looking for things to boost the morale around here you should know that the engagement on some of the teams is low. If we could plan some fun stuff like we used to do, it would be a good idea."

"Like you used to do?"

"There was a fire a few years ago here, in 2016. Lots has changed since then, but for us workers, things stalled after. It swept through the entire region, shut operations down, burned homes, work camps, and 80,000 people were evacuated for a month until things settled, and some of them much longer because their homes had to be rebuilt. The place was divided, communication with workers was hard to organize. Things haven't been the same since."

"Yes, I remember that fire. It was massive. Was there counselling and support for people after?"

"Loads of it. The recovery was handled well, or as well as it could be. But people are still suffering, you know? The pipeline of drugs coming in here is worse. It's not the place it was. The place it should be."

"Did they ever say what started that fire?"

"The official word was it was caused by people."

"What kind of people?"

He shrugged. "Officially they said it was an unintentional thing. Like the spark off a vehicle triggered a brush fire and it just took off from there." He paused, and Morgan looked at him closely. His gaze was steady, and his blue eyes were clear. His love for his home was undeniable.

"What do you think? Unofficially?" she asked carefully.

"I don't think about these things. I lost my house and we rebuilt it, just like we rebuilt the businesses, my kids' hockey rink, and the doctor's office. I do my job, and I don't like to look for trouble."

As he prepared to leave, Jack paused and rubbed his hand on his chin as if making a decision whether to say more, or leave the subject alone. Finally, he offered, "If you want to know more about what didn't officially happen, talk to Jeff Autumn. He owns the helicopter company just outside of town, Aristade Choppers, and he probably knows more than you want to."

Morgan opened a browser on her phone and did a search for Jeff's company phone number. It didn't take long to find, and she tapped the dial button.

"Look, I get what you're saying, that people want more fun at work. I'm just not sure how you knowing what happened with that fire will help you improve morale," Jeff said coolly into the phone.

"It's a piece of background I need if I am going to be able to help. Can I come speak with you at work? Would that be better than doing this over the phone?"

"Suit yourself," Jeff replied, "I'm here all day."

Morgan stared at the screen of her phone as the call was disconnected before she could say thank you or goodbye. *This guy is going to be interesting,* she thought.

Morgan confirmed with Alix that no one else was around and waiting for her, and then headed to the cafeteria to find Jake. He was sitting with his head leaning against the wall, dozing, his feet up on a chair opposite him. He opened his eyes as she approached.

"How's the job hunt honey?" she said sweetly.

"It's an interesting place, and I can start next Monday if I can get a police check done," he said with a wink. "Apparently, they need someone who can set up tighter security on their computers and peripherals."

"So, you're done here for today?"

"Yup. Just drinking shitty coffee while I wait for you."

"Good, grab your parka. We're going on a field trip."

"Where? What?" Jake said, intrigued with the idea of something to do.

Jeff Autumn shook his head when he saw Morgan. "You're here on your honeymoon? How nuts is that?"

"Well, it's a working trip, and my husband had some time to kill so we figured coming up together would be interesting. Not a conventional honeymoon, but that's okay."

She smiled her most charming smile at Jeff, as she sat across from the small desk in his office. Jake was left to fend for himself, looking at the maps and charts hanging all over the outer office. There was a good selection of aerial photos, plus the receptionist to keep him company.

"Miss, can you show me where the fire of 2016 was on these pictures?" he smiled at her.

"Just as soon as I fix my computer," she said. "I'm having problems sending an email. It keeps hanging up on me."

"Hanging up? Are you trying to use a satellite link?"

"Yeah," she said. "It's a pain to use."

"Well, you're in luck," he said. "I'm pretty good at this stuff. Want me to take a look?"

Jeff was not so easy to sweet talk as his receptionist was. "I just want to know the real reason you are asking about the fire, Mrs. Career Counsellor."

"I'm asking because since I got here, it's been mentioned a few times along with a couple of other things, and I got to thinking that perhaps there is more going on. It's impacting the morale of the people at the site where I'm working, but there are other ripples, you know? Like a guy at the bar who said that you have to either get fired from a job here or die in order to leave."

"Who are you working with at the site? Which site are you on?"

She gave him Patricia's name and went on to explain. "When I was Googling around for some details, I saw you quoted in the paper as saying that the fire started on a day when there was no lightening in the forecast, and it was in an out of the way place. There were power lines in the area where the fire started, as well as a long dry spell, hot temperatures, and you said the previous winter lacked snow. It was an objective description, but I got the impression there was more to the theory. There was no confirmation of arson or a deliberate act that I saw."

He squinted his eyes slightly, wary of where her questions were going, and answered her with a question of his own, "And you need to know this why?"

She repeated her HR story. Then she took another tack. "Look, part of my contract here involves figuring out what makes people tick, and how to engage them at work. The community has been traumatized and it seems like people are suspicious even though that fire was a few years ago. The horrific way that the police detachment commander died isn't going to help. And the changes to the Canadian and US political environment probably haven't helped either."

"Back up a sec. You know about Sheridan?"

"My husband and I were supposed to meet with him the morning he was killed."

Jeff paused, then said, "Sheridan was a good person. His kids and my kids grew up together. What were you meeting him about?"

"The fire," she lied smoothly. No need to let this guy know everything, and he was being a bit of a jerk anyway, Morgan thought.

Jeff took a deep breath and let it out slowly. "Look, I don't really know who you are or what you're up to and I'm not totally sure you won't share this online or something, or use it to bring some flashy Hollywood star up here, so I'm going to ask you not to say or print anything without asking me if it's what I really meant, okay?"

"Deal."

"The fire started well outside of Fort McMurray, that's true. The weather was dry, and it spread quickly because the conditions were perfect for it once it had a start. But when we say it was caused by humans there was evidence that was obvious by the fact it was missing, okay, not because it was there."

"Go on."

"We never found the person – or vehicle – that was responsible. Nobody ever came right out and said they were in the woods that day and they started something or saw anything. There was nothing."

"Is that unusual?"

"Yes, because normally when there is a fire that's accidentally set, we find stuff. Sometimes it's a witness. Sometimes it's the person responsible, or their spouse. A big fire like this, I expect that somebody eventually comes out of the woodwork and says they were there. They made a mistake, whether it was throwing a cigarette butt or not extinguishing their campfire, or they took a dirt bike in over low shrubs and maybe there was a spark. But we got nothing. Then, as the beast – that's what we called the fire – spread, things went horribly wrong. We knew it was heading into Fort McMurray, and so we evacuated people north to Anzac, but they got trapped by flames. And people trying to evacuate south got cut off by more flames. People died. Not a lot, the government said, but those were people, y'see? Our people. And animals. There were animals trying to run down the highway to escape and you could see smoke coming off their bodies. But there were no witnesses to the start of it, no admissions of guilt, or stupidity."

"So, do you think there was someone responsible for deliberately starting the fire? And maybe accelerating it in some places?"

He sighed, and suddenly looked tired. *Maybe he's not really a jerk,* Morgan thought. *Maybe he is plain worn out.* "Jeff, I want to help you," she said.

He looked at her, and then, perhaps taking in how she sat leaning toward him, her eyes dark and serious, the muscles in her upper arms just a little too big to hide under the corporate style suit, he nodded once, quickly, and got to his feet.

"There should be some pictures here I can show you. Hang on." He went out to the reception area, and invited Jake to come back into the office with him, since Jake was looking at the images they needed.

"These burn images are not like anything I've seen before," Jake said, throwing a glance to Morgan.

"What do you mean?" said Jeff, leaning in toward Jake.

Jake pointed at the map, "These areas here and here are off track a bit and the zoomed images show them as having burned, but they don't quite fit with the surrounding burn patterns. Like, maybe those areas were started on purpose. See how they aren't quite connected to the rest of the blackened ground?"

"Your husband's got a good eye," Jeff said, looking at Morgan.

"Yes, he does," she said agreeably.

"Ex-military I'm guessing." Jeff said, squinting at Jake for a closer look. "Want to move up here and fight some fires? Both of you?"

"Tell me more," Morgan said.

"We don't know anything," Jeff said, slumping back into his chair with a sigh. "The trail completely dried up after the fire. I'm not surprised...we were in disaster mode. Evacuations, clean up, extensive safety concerns for residents, and we did months of fire fighting that year."

"So, what're your thoughts on espionage or arson?"

"Espionage?" Jeff said. "Who brought that up?"

"I did," Morgan said. "Just now. On account of the funny lines on your aerial photos."

"Well, we certainly looked at arson, but not espionage. Not sure if it even matters now. The fire is out and the trail's gone cold, so to speak." Jeff offered. "One of our local politicians received threats after that fire, though the threats were chalked up to people being upset. There were a few high profile folks who died during the evacuations, too. Two site managers from different oil companies, a drug overdose in a place where some of our workers come from, plus there was a suicide in Edmonton. Isn't that just too many coincidences?"

Jeff paused for a moment, collecting his thoughts and then said it straight out: "Are you guys cops by any chance? Because if your bullshit story about HR and a honeymoon is really a cover for some kind of investigation, I'm all for it."

"Good," said Jake. "We can help each other out then. What's your surveillance equipment like? I'm talking night vision cameras, sound equipment, and computer access. I'd like to do some hacking and there's nowhere here that's secure enough."

CHAPTER 13

The following day, Jake dropped Morgan off back at Walterwell. She pecked him on the cheek, and said, "Have a good time on your tour of the hangar with Jeff."

"Oh, I will," he said. "It looks like a beautiful day to fly."

"You're flying?"

"Yup, he promised me a ride in a chopper if the weather was good. Looks good to me." He leaned over to kiss her again, just in case anyone was watching, and she kissed him on the lips. She pulled away slightly breathless, and Morgan said, "Be careful up there, okay. I have a funny feeling."

"What kind of feeling? Like funny ha ha, or funny leading up to a nightmare?"

"I don't know yet. Just be careful."

Morgan stopped at the cafeteria for a coffee, trying to shake the weight that settled on her shoulders when Jake said he and Jeff were taking a helicopter ride. She stirred the cream and sugar slowly, and then looked around for a bin to toss the wooden stir stick away.

"I don't think I've seen you here before," a man in work coveralls and oversized winter boots said, sounding friendly.

"I'm helping Patricia out for a few days," she said. "I was here yesterday, and I'm trying to get the lay of the land. Do you see a bin here anywhere?"

"A bin?" he smiled from ear to ear. "You from out east? Most people around here call it a garbage can."

"I just arrived from Halifax."

"Thought so," the man said, giving her a nod. His lined face crinkled into a smile, and his brown eyes glittered. "It takes one to know one."

"I guess it does," she laughed.

"Listen," he said quietly, "that's great you are helping out the team in HR. I think they need it. Just be careful though, won't you? The drugs and booze up here are a terrible thing, eh."

"Drugs and booze in HR?"

He shrugged. "Just keep yer wits about you if you're only here a few days. You'll make good money, but someone will want you to spend it."

"I thought these camps were dry and there was zero tolerance for that," Morgan said quietly, with a question in her voice.

"Sure, that's the rules," he confirmed. "But if yer stayin' in town, they're everywhere, and available 24/7. Anyone that's got any bit of weakness in 'em can't avoid it."

"Thanks, uh, what's your name?"

"It's Bert," he said, raising his coffee in salute. "Bert Holmes from Sydney, Nova Scotia."

"Thanks Bert. I really appreciate it."

Returning to the office, Morgan was happy to see Patricia was there already.

"One meeting I did yesterday was with a man who says morale is low, and it has been since the fire of 2016. What do you think of that?" Morgan said.

"He's right," Patricia said, chewing lightly on her bottom lip. "I mean, people were scattered and then coming back to their homes with all kinds of loss. Some idiot started a house fire in a neighbourhood that had been spared in the initial fire. We slept in a gymnasium in a place called Fort Saskatchewan for two weeks, me and my husband, Mike. He got called back up here pretty quick, and I was not far behind him and our house didn't burn down completely, but it still smells like smoke in there when it rains. It was like being in a war zone." she paused, and tilted her head as she recalled the memories. "But you know what?"

"What?" Morgan leaned in to hear Patricia, because the older woman's voice had dropped to a whisper.

"There were people on the news and social media saying that since the fire was in Alberta, we'd be okay. They said we lived in a wealthy province with plenty of resources and we didn't need help, and that was so wrong. It was desperate up here. We evacuated more than 80,000 people from this community. We didn't know where they went for days…some wanted to come back right away and others decided they wanted to start over. We were living in a disaster, but not anything like what you saw on TV. It was real." Patricia's pale blue eyes went vacant as she returned to the trauma in her mind. She touched the bun at the back of her head, and tiredly tucked a chunk of dyed blond hair behind her ear.

"You must've been exhausted." Morgan offered.

"I'm still exhausted. You know, the companies and the government were all talking about helping, and they did at first. But after a few weeks, their money and support suddenly ended. They were concerned with getting up and running, and getting the bitumen moving with no excuses. Leaves were cancelled. No more counselling. No more people available to rebuild. And then this new 'relationship' with the US started and there was even more trouble around with drugs and crime when we relaxed the rules on American workers coming into Canada. But we needed workers to meet their demands. Now we're getting loads of pushback about the new pipelines that should already have been built. I don't know if I'll ever stop wondering what else could go wrong around here."

"What do you mean?"

"I mean that this fire and all the other changes have altered me right to my very core. I'm not the same person I used to be, Morgan. Not the same at all."

CHAPTER 14

"So, we're talking about some kind of environmental plot, and drugs, we've got bodies and fires, and no answers." Morgan said, rubbing her forehead with the palm of her hand.

"I think," Jake said stretching his legs on the hotel bed and tucking his hands behind his head, "I will be able to figure things out after a nap."

"Knock yourself out, Jake. You've earned it."

Morgan turned away from the site of Jake's length stretched out on the bed, and called Stan. The computer chatter they had picked up about the star visit to the area, Stan reported, was really a server farm, creating havoc on the internet and although it initially appeared to be based in Russia, they had also tracked activity to Ukraine and, the most surprising place of all, smack dab in the middle of Lunenburg, Nova Scotia.

"Lunenburg? What the hell's the draw for Lunenburg?" Morgan wondered out loud. Why would that heritage town, a highly popular tourist spot, be a hotbed for online trickery, and internet spying? She glanced over at Jake stretched out on the bed and her heart caught in her throat. God, he was handsome, and the way he had fallen asleep with his body relaxed on the bed with his hands behind his head he looked ready to be taken advantage of, she thought. Then another thought sprang to mind: Jake, somewhere in a huge old library digging around stacks of books, though not in any danger. She shook her head and the image cleared.

"Follow the money, Stan. Let's see where that gets us, if there is some. If it's not cash, they have to be using some kind of digital transfers like bitcoin or cryptocurrency, maybe PayPal, I don't know, but somewhere there has to be money moving around this stuff."

She disconnected, then turned in the chair to look at Jake again. He hadn't moved. His stubbled chin was relaxed, and his hair was a curled mess on top of his head. Feeling tired herself she was tempted to catnap, but she didn't want to lay alongside him because that would be a distraction with a capital D. *By gad*, she thought in her best Maritime accent, *he was sure easy on the eyes.* She laid on the small sofa, with her head propped onto what was probably a filthy hotel pillow, and her feet up on the opposite arm rest. How Jake was managing to sleep on here at night was anyone's guess, she thought.

Thirty minutes later, Morgan jolted awake. She'd been watching that nightmare rerun again, the one where she was trying to pull her husband from the flaming plane wreckage only it wasn't her husband's face, it was Jake's. The backs of her knees were sweating, and she was stiff. She turned her head to see Jake staring at her from the bed.

"That's not creepy at all, to have you staring at me as I wake up," she said groggily.

"You were restless and I was watching over you, not staring at you. I was concerned and torn between letting you kill the demon in your sleep or waking you and having you punch me in my handsome face."

"I have bad dreams all the time. Don't worry about it."

"Was that a plane crash nightmare?"

"Yes...sort of."

"Hmm. How do you feel about helicopter rides? I just got a text from Jeff and there is someone around here who spotted something where there shouldn't be anything. He thought we may need to check it out."

"Check it out or just have a ride in a helicopter?"

"Yes," he clapped his hands together loudly, "How exciting. Let's go for a ride."

Morgan may have dragged her feet just slightly as she headed to the bathroom. *Yes indeed,* she thought, *instead of riding in some rickety twin engine plane, being in a helicopter sounds infinitely better.*

She looked at the bags by the door. "What're we taking with us exactly?"

"Oh, this is not some fire spotting ride, Morgan. This is a clandestine sweep taking place in a super stealthy helicopter that's a newer addition to Jeff's fleet. I've got the gear I borrowed from Jeff."

Morgan was intrigued. She considered that flying around might not be so bad after being jolted awake from her nap.

An hour later, they were airborne near the spot Jeff had heard about. There was a Quonset hut the size of a small airplane hangar, plus a couple of outbuildings. Morgan pulled out her night scope and zoomed in.

"Jeez, look at this place. It's a permanent camp."

Jeff had explained that if he got directly overhead it was possible someone on the ground might detect the vibration from the chopper, so he stayed back a respectable distance, hovering just at the top of the trees.

"Jeff, can you swing around the other side so we can see it from there too?" Morgan asked. Her heart was pounding in her ears from the rush of being airborne, and the confirmation that something was most surely going on. The flashes of her dream came back to her brain, unbidden. Trouble. This was trouble for sure.

From the North side of the camp, there were several snowmobiles lined up alongside the building, as well as a tarp that had blown out of the way on one end, revealing a pair of ATVs, the all-terrain vehicle preferred for off road driving.

"How would they get equipment and supplies up here without being noticed?" Jake asked. "They are out here practically in the middle of nowhere, but stuff has to come from somewhere."

"They are probably hiding it alongside stuff that's coming up here for the oil companies. There are plenty of big rigs that come up here every single day," Jeff said.

"Do you think they are using a chopper, too? There looks like a big enough space to land something in the clearing just there," Morgan said.

"Could be," Jeff said.

"Who spotted this place and told you about it, Jeff?" Morgan asked.

"A guy named Mike Buford. He works on one of the sites and said they were out doing some hunting and stumbled across this place."

"He must be married to Patricia Buford, the woman I'm working with." Morgan said. "How'd he come to tell you about it?"

"He knows I like to know what's going on, and that as fire rescue we need to know where any camps are. This one was new to him, and it's new to me...why?"

"Just wondering," Morgan said.

"Mike and Pat are good people. There are lots of good people here about," Jeff said.

"Well someone's not," Jake said into the headset loudly, then yelled, "Sharp bank Jeff, get us out of here." There wasn't time to say anything else before a bullet struck the floor beneath them and went right through Jeff's leg.

"Oh crap! Shit," Jeff yelled, banking sharply. "My new chopper!" A second bullet thunked as it came through the floor and lodged into the roof.

"Do you need help? I can see blood on your leg. Where'd the bullet go?" Jake was yelling into the headset.

Morgan's headset crackled as she called out, "It's in the ceiling. Thank God it didn't go through to the rotors. Jeff, how can I help?" she said, reaching for a first aid kit.

"F...fuck, that...that burns," Jeff said. "I thought a clean shot wasn't supposed to hurt?"

"Jeff, tell me what you need me to do. You showed me how to land yesterday, is it the same in this chopper?" Jake said, unbuckling himself.

"Yeah," Jeff said as his teeth started to chatter. "...'zact same."

Morgan wrenched open the first aid kit, and pulled a fat package off the top. She tore at the wrapper to expose the sterile pad on the inside as she passed it forward to Jake. Her hands were clammy, and she started to shake as she opened a second bandage from its wrapper and handed it forward. Jake grabbed hold of her wrist as she passed it to him, and held on.

"You're going to be okay," he said, looking at her directly and holding her gaze. Morgan replied by nodding once. She heard, but she didn't believe him.

"I'm not okay, I am definitely not okay," Jeff yelled as he heaved and prepared to throw up.

"Not on the instruments, Jeff, turn and barf in the space here." Jeff did as he was told, and Jake pried the man's fingers off the stick, reaching over to unbuckle his harness at the same time.

"Jeff, you've got to get into the back. Morgan, pressure on the wound, both sides please," Jake said through clenched teeth.

"Stay focussed Jeff. How far are we from the hangar?" Morgan asked.

Jeff began to huff as he breathed, like a woman in labour. "I could pass out. If I pass out, just find somewhere to land and then get me to the...to the...frickin' hospital."

"Morgan, do you think there is room to park this thing at the hospital?" Jake's voice was calm and warm in her headset.

"I know if there is you will find it. That'd save us a lot of time."

Jake could see the lights of the city off in the distance. "Morgan...can you call ahead and let them know we're coming in?"

"Not right now, Jake. Pretty busy here, and your patient is unconscious."

"We need to tell them we're coming." Jake repeated, his eyes on the panel looking for a radio switch to call the hospital.

"Not passed out." Jeff said with his eyes closed and a feeble wave of his hand. "I'm okay..." he said, then turned his head and heaved. Morgan eased him onto his side, so he wouldn't choke, and adjusted his head so he could stay there for a minute. She wiped some of his blood off her hands and onto her jeans, then pulled her phone out of her pocket.

"Okay Siri," she yelled, but got no response. "Siri...oh fuck. Damned phones. Jeff what's your emergency number here? Is it 911? Something else?"

Jeff didn't reply. She looked at his leg and applied pressure with her left hand while dialling 911 with her right.

"911 Operator. What's your emergency?"

"I'm in a helicopter flying into Fort McMurray. I need to know where to land at the hospital."

There was a pause as the operator started her notes. "There is no helipad at that hospital. It's still under construction. You'll need to land at the airport and we can get an ambulance to you."

"We are transporting someone with a gunshot wound and he is unconscious. We are landing at the hospital." Morgan said firmly.

"I repeat there is no helipad there. There is no place to set a helicopter down safely. You...you can try to land in the parking lot but watch out for power lines. Stay on the line and I'll advise the emergency staff at the hospital."

"Jeff are you awake? This is Morgan. Jeff, wake up." She felt for a pulse in his neck, it was weak and fast.

"Jake how much further? He isn't responding," Morgan said.

"I can see lights for Fort Mac up ahead," Jake said.

"Can you get his vital signs?" the operator asked.

"Not easily," Morgan said. "He is shot in the leg, in the right thigh, and he is bleeding heavily. I have pressure on it, but badly. The bullet went right through. His pulse is weak. He has thrown up twice. Currently unconscious."

The next five minutes stretched out in front of her. Morgan reached into the first aid bag for the last of the pads and piled it on top of the soaked ones on the top of Jeff's leg.

"Just approaching the hospital now. Heading for the corner of the parking lot with no power lines." Jake said.

Morgan tried to rouse Jeff. "Jeff, this is a good time to wake up. Jeff, help Jake land this thing so we can get you into the hospital."

"Steady yourself," Jake called out. "We're about to land."

The landing was hard. Morgan lost her grip on her phone and Jeff's leg. His eyelids fluttered.

"Jeff if you are faking, I am going to kill you when this is all over," she said through gritted teeth, watching her phone slide into his vomit.

Jake had the door open quickly, and the emergency staff were running across the parking lot with a gurney. Morgan helped manoeuvre Jeff's limp body to the door as they maneuvered him onto the stretcher. The hospital staff whisked Jeff away, over bumps of snow and ice.

"You alright?" Jake yelled as he reached to steady Morgan where she sat on her haunches just inside the door. The rotors were still spinning overhead, and the noise swallowed his yell.

"Fine, but let's try not to repeat that," she yelled back. It took all the strength that was left in her legs to get to the shotgun seat and buckle in for the trip back to the hangar.

CHAPTER 15

Two hours later, after returning the chopper, Morgan and Jake sat at the hospital. They were both alert and wary. Jeff was in surgery, and Jake had words with the hospital administrator to ensure that anyone calling the hospital with questions about the chopper or a shooting would get directed to him.

"They knew we were coming to look at that place, or they have some kind of tracking equipment on that property," Morgan said quietly. "How else could they detect a chopper they couldn't see or hear?"

"I saw a glint of light off a spotting scope right before the shot," Jake confirmed. "They were either walking around with rifles watching for Jeff, or came out of the building on a random chance. If they're trying to hide something big, then it'd make sense that they are armed to the teeth and want to take out anyone who could get in their way."

"Mike Buford?" Morgan asked. "But why? He and Jeff are friends, or at least neighbours. I don't get it."

Jake shrugged as if to say, "Who knows?"

Morgan borrowed Jake's cell, since hers was in dire need of a clean up and might never be the same again. She moved down the hall to call Stan, and told him to run background checks on Mike and Patricia Buford, along with Jeff. She also asked him to look for aerial photos, and particularly anything infrared, of the site.

"You look like shit," Jake said as she returned.

"Well, you smell like puke," she laughed at him. They sat for a moment with their heads leaning against the wall. Morgan thought back to her nap on the couch. It felt like a week ago rather than just a few hours.

"Your friend will recover," said the surgeon, much later. "We've stitched him all up. He's going to have trouble walking for several weeks, but you saved his leg. The bullet clipped an artery and we had to give him four litres of blood, which is a lot, but he's in recovery now. You can come see him tomorrow if you'd like."

"Doc, we're just waiting to put a guard on his room and then we'll clear out," Jake said quietly.

They weren't waiting for just any guard. Jake had told Morgan he had a pal that had been causing havoc in Seattle, and could stop in Fort Mac on his way home to Scotland if she felt it would help. She did. Stan made the arrangements so that Malcolm would be there at first light.

CHAPTER 16

Morgan looked at Jake, who looked at Malcolm. "So, we are most definitely looking at some kind of cell that's operating here in the area, and is hopefully being lead by a bunch of nutters, but we still haven't ruled out an international terror threat," she said.

"Okay," Malcolm acknowledged, as he sipped a beer in their hotel room.

"And we know that some of them are here working in Fort McMurray but on temporary foreign worker visas from a couple of key places, but mostly recruited through the US."

"Aye." Malcolm said. He was older than Morgan had expected an agent to be. At least 60, judging by the extensive lines on his forehead and around his mouth. His hair was salt and pepper, short but not military looking. He was not much taller than Morgan, but the muscles bulging at the end of his rolled sleeves and pressing the denim of his jeans told the story of someone lean and strong.

"Alright, so if we've found where they are from, and it's about environmentalism and oil, who is paying them? If they are working jobs up here, their average age is in the early 30s and the average income is around $90 or $100k per year. While that's not bad money, it's not enough to support themselves plus launch a major initiative. And remember we've got drug busts that took place up here. We still don't know if we are looking at a drug issue, or a combined problem for the oilfields."

"Well," Malcolm said, handing out another round of beer. "We found a cell of odd people working out of Indiana, where we were picking up all sorts of internet chatter about causes and rebellion once we decrypted it, and it was mixed messages about squashing pipeline projects, actively stopping fracking, and the like. They've been backing some huge demonstrations to stop all energy projects, especially related to pipelines and fracking."

"They raise money through donations that look legit." Stan's voice said over the speaker phone. "Like, you think you're helping save a poor kid with cancer, or a teenager to launch a cool business, or you're sending a superstar up to have a look around and then take a bunch of pictures that make everyone look bad. They create compelling, heart rendering, tear jerker stories and load them up on crowd funding sites complete with videos and stats and promises...but it's all being set up by these folks sitting behind a computer. And they collect money like it's going out of style. We even found paid ads you click on Facebook that'll take you to a spot where you can make a donation. And people do, they send bags of money to these causes."

Jeff had his recovering leg propped on an upside down garbage bin. "It seems like they somehow decided that all things related to pipelines originate in Fort McMurray, well more accurately, the Wood Buffalo region. They thought they could bring things to a halt by burning the entire region to the ground in 2016, but they didn't count on the strength and tenacity of the people living here. Then they tried to infiltrate through the drug trade, but we still don't know how much of the territory they got, because the drug gangs are working real hard for that same turf."

Morgan started counting off stats on her fingers, "So we know that the two goons who followed Jake and I in Halifax were hired by this group. Then there was the hooligan at Spray Harbour who also killed the hotel clerk, but he died waiting for the police who were busy looking at the two goons and the dead hotel clerk. The goons could have been hired as security from the operation in Lunenburg, which is a click farm. We still aren't quite sure who hired Magrath or killed

Sheridan, but it seems connected to all this. We know they are the ones who took shots at Jeff's helicopter."

"And shot me, don't forget," Jeff added.

"Yes, of course Jeff. I can't ever forget that," Morgan said. And we know that since the fire and the chaos of reconstruction there were two big drug busts quite quickly afterward, but anything since then has been minor. And we know that there is a camp just 30 kms away where they are hiding something."

"But it does seem as though these guys – including the ones in Halifax – are somewhat organized...they've got access to equipment and weapons. They're obviously getting paid, so maybe that's where the drug money was being directed." Jake said.

Morgan rubbed her temple, trying to be subtle about it but trying to clear the vision she saw of Jake in flames again. "So, our next step is to do some reconnaissance on that camp and find out what the hell they are up to. And it's winter, so grab your woollies guys. We don't want anyone freezing out there."

Jake pulled up some updated aerial photos that were taken from a satellite in the last 72 hours.

"There seems to be two different routes they take to get into their site, although it's easy to see that they are all either coming from Fort McMurray or nearby. We found a trail head here," he pointed, "and another here where they can park a vehicle and hike into the camp about 1000 metres, or they can hop on snowmobiles to get in."

"We've got a plane coming in tonight with six guys on it, highly trained members of the agency. They are all ex-military. They will be our boots on the ground, plus me and Morgan makes eight. Malcolm, you're in charge of security, so you will be located at the hangar with Jeff."

"I've heard you are a very good shot," Malcolm said with a nod to Morgan.

Morgan started to reply, but Jake jumped in. "She's a crack shot plus she's smart as hell."

"Right then, let's get on with it." Malcolm said, with a quick wink to Morgan.

Morgan looked at Malcolm, and choked back a laugh as Jake cuffed Malcolm in the back of the head. A few minutes later, Morgan found herself alone with Jake.

"Why'd you smack Malcolm?" she asked. "Do you guys normally hit each other?"

"I didn't want him crossing the line and I felt he was close to it. I like Malcolm, and have trusted him with my life several times, but he thinks he's a lady's man." Jake shook his head slowly. "He's an ass when it comes to women."

"You jealous that your ol' pal is hitting on me, Rory," she said, addressing him by his last name for the first time.

"Oh yes," he said smiling his green eyes at her.

"Don't worry, he's too old for me," Morgan winked at him.

Morgan was concerned about the size of the Buford operation, and wanted some additional help since they were so isolated. Jeff introduced her to a troop of rangers from Fort McKay, where Commander Sheridan was originally from. They all lived, hunted, and trapped in the North while also providing part time para-military and security assistance to the community when the need arose. In addition to six men, the rangers came with a half dozen snowmobiles to get around effectively.

Morgan looked at her team of special ops agents and rangers assembled at Jeff's hangar. "Starting now and for the next 48 hours, you are committed to telephone silence and this operation. We need your help, and we need to get information on a remote site. We can't risk any information leaking out or being picked up by someone who might be listening in."

"You need Paul on your advance team," the sergeant of the rangers said. "He has been in those trees practically since he was born and he moves like the wind. He's an excellent shot. He is also my son."

"Thank you, Sergeant," Morgan said. Paul Smallwood's name had already been put forward as a scout, and Morgan had reviewed his file. He was brand new out of training, but a crack shot and in peak physical condition. "Paul, are you ready?"

She looked at his face as he signalled his readiness. He is maybe 20 years old. *Far too young for real trouble like this,* Morgan thought to herself, but his gaze is steady. His body language showed him to be fit, aware, and holding on to a little tension that would serve him well today.

After spending the night putting mufflers on the snowmobiles, concealing headlamps, and testing the snow, they prepared to leave the staging area behind Jeff's hangar. There were just five of them heading out in the advance party. Smallwood, Morgan, Jake, and two special ops agents: Anderson and Selinski. The group was quiet and serious as they donned their gear.

"Okay troops," Morgan said, "It's warmed up a bit which is good. Right now, it's about minus 18 Celsius and the high for today is minus 12 with no wind anticipated, but maybe some snow flurries. This could be perfect for what we need but it means we will have to hike a bit farther so that the sound of our snowmobiles doesn't give us away. Maintain radio silence and use hand signals when possible. You are wearing sophisticated headgear, so you should be able to speak very quietly to one another or to the entire team, even within a fight situation. Remember that and don't yell. You should be heard at a whisper. We expect that the area closer to the site could be boobie trapped and there will be cameras. They will be expecting us to some degree and we don't want to engage anyone in a battle. This is reconnaissance only. Keep safe. This is not a drill. Let's all get back in one piece tonight, with all the information we need."

Jeff watched from the window as the advance team assembled. "Is it bad that my leg is a mess and I'm grateful not to be on that excursion." Malcolm shook his head no, poured two coffees, and sat down to wait. The rest of the special ops team and rangers set up a security rotation for the hanger, then entertained themselves by working out or playing cards. They were used to situations of hurrying, intense action, and then waiting. This one was no different.

Instead of slinging rifles and snowshoes on their bodies, the recce team had packs bundled to the back of their snowmobiles. They each had a spare automatic rifle, a handgun, ammo, knives, and snowshoes. For provisions they kept things very simple and carried a small supply of fortified water, and protein bars.

Their snowmobiles could reach high speed on open ground, but in the woods they would be restricted by the forest and underbrush. After an hour and a half, Smallwood raised his left arm like a cyclist signalling a turn, and they followed his lead to a hunter's cabin. This cabin hadn't been seen on the aerial views because of the dense cover provided by the trees above, but it belonged to Smallwood's family and he was very familiar with it.

The cabin was not locked to allow for a hunter or traveller who might get lost or caught out in bad weather. Smallwood checked to make sure there were no guests, and the team parked their snowmobiles in the crawl space under the deck at the back of the building. They covered the ends of the machines with a white tarp to offer some camouflage against the snow, then used branches and raked over their footprints to help hide their numbers, just in case anyone had followed them.

They would have to hike the final six kilometres on snowshoes. Everyone was alert, and aware of the need to hustle.

Morgan took a deep breath as she headed into the woods at the rear of the line. It had started to snow, and she was glad of it providing it helped their mission rather than being an obstacle.

Two hours in, after snowshoeing over rough terrain, and startling a small herd of deer, the group stopped. Anderson and Selinski spoke quietly with Smallwood and watched closely as he climbed a small hill to scope out the way ahead. He returned with an all clear, and the team finished eating their protein bars before moving on.

About 1000 metres from Buford's camp, Smallwood signalled the team to stop and they all squatted down on their haunches. He pointed up in the trees where, well above eye level they could see signs of a digital perimeter. If they proceeded as planned, they were certainly going to get caught on camera. If they waited for darkness, however, the trek out would be dangerous.

Morgan backed away slightly from the group. She hit send on a message that was on her satellite phone and would tell Malcolm exactly where they were. Jake had set up some interference that Malcolm would turn on once he had the coordinates, allowing the bad guys to see an old loop on their cameras while the team moved into the area. The recce team waited patiently, squatting down and balancing on their heels to stay low in the woods, allowing their heavy rucksacks to act like a temporary cushion. Morgan was happy to see more snow falling fast, since it would quickly cover the track they had left. She shivered from the adrenaline rather than a chill, and thought how surreal these surroundings were. Here she was on a mission, despite being surrounded by Christmas snow. *A spy mission in the winter, big guns, danger. I'm trapped in a Bruce Willis movie*, Morgan thought.

A single high pitch signal in her headset told her Malcolm's tampering was done, and she signalled to the team that they were ready. Morgan and Selinski had cameras on their helmets so they could get good pictures of their surroundings. The special ops agents had done a lot of training in this kind of forest, working from time to time with the rangers. They moved ahead and kept pace with Smallwood, who was travelling at high speed yet staying silent. When the Quonset hut came into view, the team split up. Morgan and Jake moved to the north of the compound where they knew the snowmobiles and entry points from the pathways were. Anderson and Selinski stayed further south where the two outbuildings were. Smallwood, as their sniper, was to stay hidden in the shrubs for the time being and provide back up if they needed it.

Morgan and Jake stayed low. The big bay door at the end of the Quonset hut was shut tight against the weather, but to the right of it was a small man door. The door had either just been opened, or the hut was being kept very warm inside judging by the steam rolling out of the open gap.

Parked alongside the building there were 14 snowmobiles that could hold two people each, a pair of ATVs that could each carry four people, and a larger ATV that could seat eight. Morgan did the math quickly, noting the potential for the Buford's to move 44 people fast if they needed to. Under a white tarp they could see the outline of a large mounted anti-aircraft gun. The area around it looked well cared for and operational. They laid on their bellies in the snow, rifles ready and watching for movement.

It was very still as Morgan and Jake waited for signs of activity around the hut. They were quickly covered in snow but neither of them moved. After fifteen minutes, the man door opened wider and two young women in parkas, fur trimmed hats, and knee high insulated white boots emerged. They were speaking loudly, not seeming concerned about being watched or heard as they climbed onto a snowmobile and headed off to the well used trail. Morgan followed their activity closely so the images would be picked up by her camera, while Jake kept watch through his scope. In quick succession, six more people left the building, some climbing aboard shared snowmobiles, and others riding alone. They were, without exception, petite women, and though she couldn't be absolutely certain, Morgan didn't think any of them were carrying weapons or wearing any type of armour. They looked like regular people heading home after work.

Forty-five minutes later, having done a good tour around the perimeter and gathering what information they could, the team met up close to Smallwood before retreating deep into the woods.

They were three quarters of the way back to the hunter's cabin before anyone spoke into their headset. Selinski whispered that they got pictures of the outbuildings. One seemed to be a small shed for storage, but no indication what was in it though lots of tracks that people went in and out. The other was obviously for smoking fish, judging by the smell.

"Fish?" Smallwood whispered. "For sure?"

"Looked like it," said Anderson, agreeing with Selinski. "Smelled like a smoker."

"That'd be really odd to be smoking fish there."

"You mean it's probably hiding something else, Smallwood?" Jake's voice was thoughtful.

"I would say so, I mean I don't know for sure. These all look like southerners and so it's hard to know what they'd do, but I don't know what it was there for."

"Southerners?" Jake repeated.

"Yeah," Smallwood said. "People come from the south to work up here. Southerners. The ones I saw leaving weren't like you white people, though. They are smaller, probably from the Philippines."

CHAPTER 17

As they approached the cabin to collect their snowmobiles, the group slowed. They could see ATV tracks and footprints. Smallwood and Anderson approached the building slowly, while Selinski went around the back. Whomever had been there was long gone given by the amount of snow collected in the tracks, or they were hiding.

Morgan heard a boom, right before feeling a rumble under her feet. She turned just in time to see Jake land behind her, tossed into a soft shrub by the blast. There was a track of flame stretching toward his resting spot, but it was sputtering in the snow. Morgan ran to Jake and extended an arm to help him out of the shrubbery. They took a few steps and he stumbled, dazed from being knocked off his feet. She looked for a place to help him sit down when they heard another boom from the other side of the deck. This one shook the cabin.

"Check in," Morgan said into her microphone. Everyone counted off back to her. They were all fine. Looking around her slowly, she realized that this was the scene from her premonition or whatever that was, where she had seen Jake surrounded by fire, the only difference being that the snow had muffled the blast from doing any real damage.

"Smallwood, any sign of anyone who has been here tampering?" she said into the headset.

His voice shaking, he said, "No visuals, but the inside of the cabin has been ransacked."

She turned to Jake, "You okay?"

"I'm fine," he said. "But that was weird."

"Weirder than usual?"

"No, it was weird because while my ears were ringing I could see you look right at me, like you were looking right through me."

"Yeah, well, I may have had a dream about this the other day, but I was missing a few details. I just knew I had to get you out of where you landed."

They both looked at the area where Jake had been, and saw the shrub burning in earnest. Anderson, Selinski, and Smallwood came around the building with shovels and axes to put it out.

"Let's get outta here," Morgan said, once they were all convinced the fire was out and there were no other dangers around.

Several hours later, they emerged from the woods on their snowmobiles, and opened the throttles on their machines to make the last leg across open ground toward Jeff's hangar. That last stretch would have been a lot more fun if they hadn't had problems at the cabin, Morgan thought. They hadn't found signs of people, or any other explosives, but the ransacked cabin and incendiaries were disturbing.

Jake saw Smallwood speaking with his Dad, and wandered over. The sergeant looked at him. "I am very proud of my son," he said.

"You should be, Sergeant. He was a very capable guide."

"He is telling me that you came across some kind of fish smoking shed at the compound, but we don't think they were smoking fish there."

"What do you think?"

"Let's go speak with your special ops people and see what they can tell me."

"Okay, okay," Sergeant said to Anderson. He turned to Selinski, "Now you describe it."

"Well Sarge, I've never been around smoking fish, but the smell reminded me of something that was being smoked. Maybe a Scotch. It had a...a peaty smell."

"Ah," the sergeant said. "You're a Scotch man. Around here we call it whisky. If you could smell smoke but not fish, it seems likely they are not smoking fish. They might be burning muskeg, though why they would do that is beyond me. It's a very damp fuel, though it can burn a long time. My guess would be that there are maybe people or equipment or something under that shed that has to be kept warm. Something precious that they are trying to protect."

"Jeez Sarge, how'd you put that together?" Jake asked.

"The benefits of watching crime shows on TV," the man said, his face serious. His hair was in wisps across his face, silver streaks among the jet black.

Morgan came into the room. "I just spoke with Stan. He still has a line into the camera system and he is recording everything."

"Can you ask him to look closely at the smoking hut. We need some insight."

Anderson approached the table. "Look at this," he said putting the photos on the table. "The heat sensor images from the satellite show the smoke shack is cooler than the hut itself. This might be some kind of exhaust, or maybe an emergency exit from the hut. The second shack has only a mildly elevated heat footprint."

"Do you think we're about to walk into something way bigger than we expect when we go into this place?" Jake asked.

"I don't know for sure, sir," Anderson said. "But to be honest, my spidy senses are tingling."

"What?"

"It's a Spiderman reference, Sir."

"It means his intuition is telling him something is wrong." Morgan asked.

"Yeah, we had Spiderman on TV when I was a kid. I just never put the two together," Jake said. "Anderson, what do you think we are heading into?"

"A mess, pretty likely. It's suspicious to your friend Malcolm that we still have access to the cameras. Those explosives at the hunting cabin were pretty mild, not seriously going to do a lot of hurt, though loud enough to tell them what time we were there. Unless we do a second recce and gather some more intel, it's hard to gauge."

"What if we set up surveillance around the entry points to the trails tonight? Let's see who and what's going in from a different perspective," Smallwood suggested.

"Can we get a couple of men up at the entrances with drones?" Malcolm piped up. "That way we can see who is entering and leaving the trails, get some pictures and whatever else we can, but no one is going to get hurt."

They set up teams for the drones – two men at each entrance to the paths coming into the site. Then they set up tight security at Jeff's hanger and at the hotel before calling it a night.

Morgan was restless, but this time she didn't wake up to a nightmare. Instead, she woke to the buzzing of her phone alarm. Jake was exiting the shower as she rubbed her eyes.

"C'mon sleepy head. It's game time," he said cheerfully.

"You don't have your contacts in yet. You can't go anywhere."

"They'll be in by the time your hair is wet."

She showered quickly, and as she blow dried her hair, Morgan said a little prayer that there wouldn't be any fistfights. She really preferred to shoot from a safe distance and avoid the hand to hand stuff if possible.

CHAPTER 18

The team at Jeff's hangar was ready 30 minutes early. The special ops agents, including Anderson and Selinski, were double checking one another's ammo supplies when Smallwood approached.

"Where's my father?" the young ranger asked. "I had to leave without him this morning."

"He's in the office with Malcolm," Anderson said. "They're looking at last night's photos."

Morgan was finishing a call with Stan. He still had access to the security cameras, and he was concerned about it. "I don't like it Morgan. They can't be ignoring their own equipment, and I'd be an idiot if I thought they didn't know we had been in there."

"Any recommendations?" Morgan asked, not wanting to hear of anything that would stop their mission.

"Not from me. I spoke with the director and he suggests you wait another day so we can gather some more intel."

"We don't have time to wait. These guys know we're here and they're busy fortifying their location. Have the director give me a call please." Delays would just mean there was more potential for people to get hurt.

"Trouble in paradise?" Jake asked, eyebrow raised.

"I was just speaking to Stan. The director's going to call me shortly. We should take the call somewhere private."

"In there," Jeff said pointing to his server room. "There's a small secure room at the back. It's built as a bunker where we can wait out any kind of fire on the ground. It's sound proof but you'll have good reception for your call."

"Morgan," the Director said using her first name. "I know you've got your hands full up there, but we're picking up very distinct chatter here today. Is it possible that the folks you are looking at have a computer room with their own spies working among them?"

"It's possible sir. Some of the employees we saw yesterday weren't dressed for any kind of manual work, and came out of the building laughing and chatting like it was just a regular job they were doing. I suppose they could be doing just about anything that will help advance their cause."

"Good, because the chatter we're picking up is all about your neighbourhood. And a Sikorsky hiding in the woods. Did you see helicopters out there? We haven't picked anything that big up on the satellites, but it looks like there is space to land something at that camp."

"No sir we haven't seen that they have one, but we suspect something similar given the space available. We are waiting to see what's there this morning."

"Keep me posted."

"Sikorsky's?" Jake said after Morgan had disconnected. "Aren't they a bit old?"

"That's just his code name for helicopters. He thinks he is being funny." She walked out into the office area, and spoke to Jeff. "Our director thinks maybe the other guys have a couple of helicopters. How many do you know of around here?"

"Well I have nine, and there is a company that does tours for the region that has four, another two at one of the oilfield companies, and two pilots at another but they rent choppers from me."

"Do you think you could raise the flag with your friends? Ask them all to be airborne in 30 minutes as a favour to create a screen for us? Then you could fly our team in as close as possible in your stealth 'copter so we can make the hike in fast?"

"Aren't you going to ask me if my leg's okay? If that chopper is fit to fly?"

"Are you looking for sensitivity Jeff? 'Cause that ended the moment you bled all over me and then I had to pick my phone out of a pile of your barf."

"Well, fine, no sensitivity from you then. I get it. I'm sorry I reacted to being mortally wounded. I don't know what came over me. And yes, I can fly you in. I'd be honoured to help. First, come check this out."

"What?" Morgan said as she headed toward the freshly painted chopper alongside Jeff.

"We've not just filled the bullet holes, but we reinforced the bottom plate with a titanium polymer paint that's not even on the market yet. I'm testing it. It should deflect most bullets, plus I've added a titanium mat around my seat."

"Right," Morgan agreed, taking a second look at the finish on the bottom of the chopper. "Very nice...and your butt is certainly protected. What about the rest of the floor?"

"Well, this stuff is expensive and still being tested, so the rest of the floor, well, it's still vulnerable if the paint doesn't work. We're just getting started with this technology, but it's cool, hey?"

"Yeah, very cool, especially if they are aiming for the pilot. Less cool for those of us sitting in the back."

"I'm sending you the bill for this by the way," Jeff called behind her as she left to gather the team. "It seems fair since I got shot working for you."

Morgan's laugh was instant and loud as Jeff limped to catch up with her.

Jeff had them to the drop zone just before sunrise. There were several choppers up and about, and Morgan thanked them all silently and made a note to remember to thank them properly when this was all done. When they landed, the sky was dark and heavy, and the air was damp. Morgan's breath, measured and slow to keep the adrenaline rush at bay, came out in cool clouds of condensation. The team gathered in line, ready to head out. Smallwood was in the lead. Sarge was at the end of the line.

Jake stood beside Morgan as the team assembled. "You okay boss?" he mouthed to her.

She gave him a thumb's up. This was a better plan, a quick entry, time to neutralize their targets, and out again. The drones had picked up lots of activity going in and out of the site last night. The access path that wasn't used yesterday by the employees was busy all night taking in supplies on the ATVs. They assumed that the supplies were weapons, and perhaps extra people.

The drones had also picked up something else. Instead of just the one they saw yesterday, there were now three large anti-aircraft guns uncovered and pointed toward the air. They had recorded the guns being loaded by hand by personnel carrying the missiles from the Quonset hut into the gun nests. Given how quickly the teams could load the missiles, it was obvious the ammunition was stacked close to the exit of the Quonset hut.

"In position," Jake's warm voice whispered in her headset.

The snow started to fall in earnest and Morgan looked to the sky. Sure, it made things hard to see for her team, but hopefully it messed up the bad guys too.

She was with Jake, and they were flanked by the special ops agents as they approached what was now being called the Buford Bunker. The rangers, who did not have close combat training, were behind their line by about five meters, ready to shoot. The only exception was Smallwood, who was lying in wait as their sniper, hidden from site in his arctic gear and branches stuck into straps along his parka to make him look like a shrub. From his vantage point on the edge of the compound, he was invisible.

Morgan signalled Jake that they head to the first gun nest. The gun started moving, taking aim directly on their position.

"Christ," Jake stage whispered. "Take cover."

The whoosh of the missile over their heads shook the ground. They watched with their mouths open as the missile seemed to lose itself in the crown of trees, and then get hung up and fall to the ground. It didn't blow up and the team looked at each other. It didn't detonate, and now there was no way to tell if or when it would.

The gun turret moved again, and Anderson bolted across the parking lot toward the snowmobiles. He pushed the ignition on one and hopped on. He'd draw fire away from the team so they could get moving.

The second missile flew true, and Morgan cringed as she saw the missile hit its target and Anderson's body flipped in the air before striking one of the giant trees. His snowmobile exploded as it hit the ground. *Oh fuck*, Morgan thought, *here we go.*

"Rory?" She used Jake's last name.

"I hear you, over."

"Rory, flank me, and let's put the plan in motion. Selinski move in for Anderson. Smallwood, are you ready?"

"Roger," said Selinski.

"Yes. A...affirmative," Smallwood said.

Morgan saw the look of fear cross the ranger sergeant's face as he heard the pause in his own son's voice.

"Sarge," Morgan said. "On my six, right now."

"Got it," Sarge said, and he moved in closely behind her.

There was movement at the man door, and the large bay of the Quonset began to open. Six women, all of them petite, but otherwise indecipherable from one another because of their balaclavas, stood evenly spaced across the open doorway. They raised their rifles to waist level, like a bunch of space cowboys, but no higher.

"They can't lift their weapons," Morgan whispered incredulously. "Their weapons are too heavy."

"Okay Smallwood, it's your turn," Jake whispered. "Make it happen."

"Roger."

Tap, tap, tap, Smallwood fired one round into each of first three shooters. The women fell to the ground in succession. The other three women began to shoot from their hips, aiming into the grove of trees across from them, but not aiming at anything better than that. Smallwood took aim again. Tap, tap, tap.

"Excellent work, Smallwood," Morgan said.

The man door opened fully and someone in tactical gear stepped up. He raised an automatic weapon. His bullets sprayed the snow caught in the shrubs and ricocheted off the trees. One of the bullets buzzed past Jake's ear, yet Jake still held his fire.

Tap. Tactical man grunted as Smallwood's bullet connected with a flak jacket. It unsteadied the man enough that he lowered one knee and prepared to fire from where he kneeled. Jake hesitated a moment not wanting to give away his position. "Wood, hit him again," Jake ordered through clenched teeth.

Tap. They saw the blood spreading from the man's nose. Smallwood had aimed just below the man's helmet and hit him below his armour. It was a master shot.

Morgan's team approached the hut cautiously, watching for a second assault to leave the building. If there were 40 people here, and they had just neutralized seven, that still left 33 unaccounted for.

The special ops group split in two, with three men headed toward the second anti-aircraft gun, and two directly heading for the smoke shack. At the smoke shack were two men behind a gun nest, their helmets poking up over a wall of sandbags that weren't there last night.

Selinski pulled a grenade from his pouch, removed the pin, and lobbed it in. He followed quickly with a second grenade, to unseat the anti-aircraft gun that stood looming. The men died screaming, their armour useless at saving their legs and arms from the blast, while blood spread quickly beneath them on the bright white snow.

Morgan moved into position on the edge of the large doorway of the hut. She could see at least four targets well inside with weapons drawn but obviously protecting the small door behind them. She sprayed the floor in front of them with bullets, not wanting a bullet to go through the closed area behind them in case the place exploded, and her bullets sent chunks of rubbery flooring up in the air, drawing fire from the four. Jake came in behind her and let loose a string of bullets exactly level with their chests. Two of them were kitted out in body armour and stumbled but didn't fall. Jake's second burst aimed slightly higher and did the job.

"Four more neutralized," he said into the headset.

"Let's get in that office," Morgan said.

Morgan could hear gunfire behind her as the special ops team moved in. A huge blast that shook the ground and made their ears ring confirmed that the helicopters hidden in the clearing were not going to be airborne anytime soon.

Morgan kicked at the office door with her boot and jumped back to avoid gunfire from the inside. The door didn't budge. She wound up and kicked again. Jake came from behind her and shot the doorknob, and Morgan shouldered the door. It gave way. Jake threw in a smoke grenade and drew back to wait.

Blam.

Smoke billowed out of the door and they could hear yelling from the inside. "No, you can't come in here. You can't destroy this!"

Morgan looked to Jake as she pulled a respirator with night vision goggles across her face. They would help her to see in the smoke. He nodded. She went through the doorway keeping low. She caught movement and fired a short burst into the middle. Brraatttattat. She retreated out the door, just as there was a thump as someone fell to the floor.

"Gun nest one neutralized," she heard in her headset.

"Four neutralized at nest two," came next.

"Is gun two ours?" Jake asked.

"Negative. The remote is not here. Repeat, the remote is not here." Whoever held the control for gun two was not at the nest. They could operate the gun from up to twenty metres away.

"Check the smoke shack," Jake said. "And be careful."

Special ops agent Cordoba drew a grenade from his belt and removed the pin. He lobbed it carefully up to the chimney, and then heard it pinging against the side as it dropped into the room below. He crouched out of the way, signalling to his partner to lay flat. The smoke shack exploded in a shower of wood and metal, and then they heard screams of the gun operator. The remote was a large laptop and it had flown out of his hands, landing near Cordoba in a shattered mess.

"Remote for gun two neutralized," Cordoba said drily.

Morgan was concerned that no one had left the office area yet. She'd only heard one thump and wasn't even sure that person was shot — they may have just been overcome by smoke, though the usual reaction to a smoke grenade was people running out of a place.

She indicated to Jake she was going back in. He jerked his head up and down in the affirmative, ready to follow. She crouched down below the level of the desk and turned on the torch attached to her scope to see through the rolling smoke. Nothing. She carefully rounded the edge of the desk and saw the outline of Patricia Buford lying on the floor. Morgan reached down to check the pulse in Patricia's neck when she felt the pressure on her parka change before registering the sensation that a bullet had hit her in her left arm. "Lucky that wasn't my shooting arm, bitch," Morgan said through clenched teeth, and she fired her weapon, killing Patricia instantly.

"You okay?" she heard Jake whisper in her headset as if he was standing next to her.

"I'm brilliant," she said, but Jake caught the slurring of her words.

"Are you hurt?"

"Only my pride," she said, and with her teeth clenched together she backed toward the door.

Suddenly a figure loomed in front of her, too close for her to fire her weapon and with her gimpy arm she couldn't reach her knife. He was wearing a mask and not slowed by the smoke. He came on quickly with a large knife raised. She raised her rifle and pushed hard against the man's groin. "Give it up now," she barked. "Or you'll end up dead like her after this bullet tears your balls off."

She felt Jake behind her suddenly, and saw his pistol through smoke beside her. "Try not to kill him. We might need one of them to fill us in on all this," Morgan yelled.

Jake sighed before firing and hitting the man in the leg, felling him.

Mike Buford groaned as he hit the floor. Jake dragged him out of the smoky office before securing the big man's hands behind him.

"Are you alright?" Jake said, looking at Morgan as he worked.

"I'm fine. It's just a graze."

"Doesn't look like a graze. You're oozing blood through your parka." He reached into his pocket for a field dressing. "Here, let me help you."

She grunted as he tied the straps around the bandage. She could smell him, he was so close and she thought briefly about falling into his arms before she pulled herself up to her full height, and cleared her throat.

With her arm secured temporarily, Morgan and Jake headed into the back half of the hut. Through a partition, in the back third, they found two special ops agents and a ranger with guns drawn on a group of women. The prisoners were on their knees with their fingers locked behind their heads as the ranger went through the group, securing their wrists together.

One woman, thin and scared, lunged at the burly ranger from where she kneeled on the floor. He was calm, and his hand shot out quickly to press on the top of her head to stop her momentum. She was olive skinned, petite, and her face was pock marked. She crumpled as she burst into tears.

"Will I be deported?" she sobbed. "I have children here. Don't take me to jail." The woman beside her started to cry, and that was enough to set off the entire group.

"Ladies, ladies," Jake said gently, holding up his right hand in a 'hold it' pose. "We are just here to stop this operation. Your questions will have to be answered by police. Please, cooperate and let's take things one step at a time."

Morgan stood in the background, impressed at how even when frightened, the group of women responded to Jake's size and demeanor. The women sniffled and sobbed as they tried to quell their crying.

She looked to the senior special ops agent for a report. They had uncovered weapons and an ammunition stash, explosives, and a small bank of computers. Morgan followed him to check it out.

"They have enough ammo here to do very serious damage," Rogers said, leading Morgan and Jake. "We found a huge storage area underneath this building. One entrance was through the outbuilding that had the smoky exhaust, but the main entrance is at the back. There's a ramp and a bay door that exits almost right into the woods. It's how they were bringing materials in, and seems to have been their main method of supplies coming in and out. This place would be a thorough disaster if someone dropped a bomb on it. There are piles of illegal drugs down there, too, under all this weapon making gear."

"Is it booby trapped?"

"Not so far."

"How were they keeping this all secure and hidden? Where the hell's their security force? I'm expecting more guys in flak jackets like the ones we saw outside."

"We did come across a few guys in one of the outbuildings. Above ground was just an entryway that led down a short flight of stairs and we knocked them out with a stun grenade. They have piecemeal uniforms on from different security companies. Probably had been fired from the oil industry somewhere else and got hired here. Judging by the garbage in their office they were drug users – we'll get it tested but there was powder and pills. They didn't put up a serious fight."

Morgan left shaking her head about how someone from special ops described a serious fight. When she saw the two security guards the agent had referred to, their faces were bloodied and one had a broken leg from falling down the stairs.

"There have to be at least 20 guys here with flak jackets and weapons like the guy we saw earlier at the man door. Where the hell are they?" she asked into her headset.

"Psst."

"Who is that?" Jake barked quietly into the headset.

"Smallwood," came a quiet whisper.

"Report," Morgan said.

"There are 15 guys in tactical gear creeping in my direction, and they are headed for the compound. They were waiting in the woods. I've moved position and I am at your six, fifteen feet up a spruce."

"Roger," Morgan said, and barked orders into the headset.

Bullets began coming into the Quonset hut as Buford's tactical unit fired from the edge of the trees into the compound, effectively pinning down Morgan's team. Buford's men had moved in because they weren't able to raise Buford on the radio, but they didn't appear to be receiving orders. They were disorganized, firing and taking cover at random.

Smallwood waited for the men to pass his position while he fixed a silencer to the end of his rifle. He shot four of Buford's men as soon as they passed his tree without giving away his position. Jake and the special ops agents scattered, and returned fire quickly and furiously.

Morgan and the rangers quickly made most of the middle of the pack ineffective. The final five bad guys fought longer, but they were no match for such expert weapons handling, and they were smart enough to avoid firing directly on the crate of anti-aircraft bombs where Morgan had her rifle resting. Soon there were no more attackers, just people lying in pools of their own blood. Some of them, like Mike Buford, still alive, but most of them ready to load into body bags.

CHAPTER 19

Jake sat next to Morgan on the aircraft. They were travelling first class thanks to an upgrade from the director, so that Morgan could keep her arm comfortable and Jake had room for his legs.

"I'll adjust to the time zone changes easier if I take it in two jumps instead of eight hours all at once," Jake said to explain why he would see her settled in Halifax before his return to Ireland.

"You just don't want to go back to work," Morgan laughed, rubbing her forearm. By the time they had wrapped up the mission, she'd lost so much blood she couldn't speak properly, and the same surgeon in Fort Mac that had fixed Jeff's leg had been the one to save her arm. Somehow, instead of bleeding like a normal person, there had been a huge amount of blood that pooled within her arm and created severe internal tissue damage. A full week after surgery, her left arm ached most of the time, and it wouldn't move no matter how hard she tried, unless she lifted her shoulder and set it going like a pendulum.

Morgan was glad to return to the place she considered home. She shut her eyes and took a few deep breaths as the plane prepared to take off for Halifax and she reviewed the last two weeks in her mind. The agency had made sure her apartment was secure, and they had taken care of the issues in Lunenburg by coordinating a small operation with the local police and military. To no one's surprise there was a drug and digital operation going on out of an old historic property in the beautiful coastal city. Hacking, embezzlement, and theft were the goals. There was evidence of Magrath getting hired from there, before he had hired the taxi and jeep drivers. The same drivers whose contracts had ended after the fight at Spray Harbour.

When Jake and Morgan arrived at her apartment, she was surprised to see a bowl of fruit and a vase of flowers on the table. Between them was a small bottle of very expensive Scotch, and a card that just had the initial "S" inside it. Stan.

Jake brought their bags in and dropped them in the entryway before returning to the car to bring in the groceries. He had promised to cook if she let him stay. She found the idea of him leaving depressing, and encouraged him to stick around.

Jake was a man of his word, and they sat together that evening with the first home cooked meal since they'd met. Jake promised it would help her heal as she tucked into his cure and his laughter filled the kitchen as she struggled to twist spaghetti onto her fork before he grabbed a knife and cut the noodles for her.

"Go on and finish that up," he said. "There are no containers for storing leftovers in this kitchen."

"That's okay," Morgan said. "You can just throw the lid on the pot and it'll fit in the fridge."

Jake frowned, "Not with my food you can't. That's sacrilegious or something."

Later they sat comfortably in front of the television, while Morgan drank a Diet Pepsi and Jake sipped the fine Scotch Stan had sent.

"That stuff you are drinking is shite you know, nothing good about it," he said.

"Yeah, but it's cold and bubbly without alcohol to interfere with my pain killers."

"Oh right. Is it time for a tablet?" he half stood, ready to go to the kitchen and grab the pill bottle.

"No, I'm stretching out the interval so I don't get hooked on them. Did you know that a lot of addicts actually start out as regular people and then get hurt at work and start taking pain pills?"

"Yeah, I've heard that."

"You know, I'm still working off the surprise that mild mannered Patricia and Mike were prepared to destroy that entire community. For that matter, they were prepared to end the oil industry as we know it. The people they were ready to kill. It's staggering."

"Yeah, I feel for that Sheridan fellow, the cop, too. What a way to go, poor bastard, all because he knew something was going on and would have found them sooner or later."

"Or he may not have found them at all," she said, rubbing her arm distractedly. "They were prepared to blow that entire area up before the spring fire lookouts started and could have almost avoided detection if they'd been a little smarter. Mike Buford chose the time to tell Jeff they were there because he knew Jeff's team would find them eventually, but he picked that time to push Jeff to react and was ready to kill him."

"You're rubbing your arm again. You're not supposed to do that," Jake reminded her gently. "You want me to help with some exercises?" He moved from the far end of the couch to sit beside her, taking her wrapped hand in between his big ones.

"No, I'm okay," she said. "I'll do the exercises."

"You'll need to do them every day," he reminded her, "or you'll be forced into retirement."

"Don't worry," she said. "I'll do them."

"You should come recuperate in Ireland," he said, rushing the words out of his mouth. "I have a great team that worked with me before, and they'd have you fixed up in no time. We could hang out."

"Hang out?" she said, sputtering. "We don't hang out. We work."

"We're hanging out right now," he said, trailing his fingers along her numb arm. "I could help you. How're you going to eat when you can't cook and you can't get to the shops for food?"

"Like I usually do," she laughed. "Delivery." She used her good hand to move her bad arm out of his way.

"I would love for you to come to Ireland and visit some castles with me."

"Why?" she looked at him earnestly. "Is there something up? You're being persistent about this and you don't need to be."

"You mean besides the fact that I am looking for ways to stay close to you?" he asked, pretending to be offended. "Actually, yes, I spoke with the director this morning. There's a job coming up and I want you with me because I need someone – preferably female – who can handle herself with a gun."

"Jake, they've told me it could be really hard for me to get this arm moving, months even. It's going to be a while before they let me back in the field."

"That's why you need to come to Ireland. It's where plenty of ex-military and security forces and spies do rehab, at a clinic north of Dublin. You can heal, work, and help me find these characters I need to look for."

"Jake, I don't know. We just got here. I'm exhausted," *though I could be ready for some hot steamy sex*, she thought.

"Of course you're exhausted. You've been hurt. But look at you, another successful mission under your belt, and aye, yes, you've got to heal. But look at James Bond, he was regularly getting his arse kicked and then taking the next assignment."

She looked at him and then laughed. "Speaking of Mr. Bond, there is a lot of, er...tension between us that we need to settle."

"Tension? You mean bad tension?"

She sighed at him, exasperated. "No idiot, the sexual tension. The kissing at the airport and on the job really rocked my socks off and I had to do some serious head games to get you out of my brain and get the work done. And now you're sitting here touching me. And, I feel a bit like Jeff whining like this, but I fucking got shot Jake. Shot. Could have died. Man, give me a break."

"Och, now back up a sec. Serious head games, you said. What's that?" He turned on the couch so he could face her. He wasn't wearing his contacts and his green eyes were bright while a smile pulled at the corners of his mouth.

"Because we had a job to do and I didn't want my feelings getting in the way of work," she said.

"Well isn't it lucky that we have both proved we can put our personal feelings aside and still get the job done," he said.

"W...what?"

"Oh come on, Morgan, you know I think you smell good. I can't stop looking at you, and making excuses to be close to you. And I must say you are a mighty fine kisser, plus you are very good in emergencies when there is blood, or bullets, or vomit flying around."

"W...well...I..."

"Aw woman," he leaned into her, "just give me a little kiss, and then see what happens."

He leaned toward her and she met him half way. She felt his warm, soft lips, as her tongue reached out for his gently.

CHAPTER 20

Six weeks later, they pulled up to the front of an Irish castle. As they drove up the narrow roadway, Morgan took in the ivy covered elegance peeking out at them from the fog.

"Aw, this is a beautiful place, Jake. I'm really starting to think I could live in a castle. Look at it."

"C'mon quick," Jake said. "Or we'll lose our seat at Cabra Castle's famous brunch."

The table linens were crisp and pressed, and the drink service was impeccable. Morgan thanked the waiter as he placed a napkin across her lap. She looked up to see Jake studying her carefully. He was wearing his hair longer these days, and it fell across his forehead almost reaching his eyes. "You've got your contacts in. You didn't have them in when we left this morning. What's up?"

"Aw nuthin'. Just doing a little scouting. The lamb here is delicious, and the Caesar salad will blow your socks off."

"It says there is blood pudding in the Caesar salad. Is that what it sounds like?"

"Oh aye, you're gonna love it. Besides, it'll help fix your arm."

Morgan snorted and held back a laugh. "I think I'll have the lamb instead. This place is some kind of fancy," she said as she took a sip of cider and looked about the dining room. There were fine china tea cups and saucers on the sideboard, and the room was decorated with knick knacks made from thin delicate china, and ceramics. One sideboard held a collection of multiple sizes of highly polished silver tea pots.

"Wait until you see the knights in their shined up armour dotted around the place."

They enjoyed their brunch, lingering over the time together like the newlyweds everyone thought they were. Afterward, they visited the parlour, where portraits of various sizes covered the walls from the ceiling down to the tops of the fancy settees and chairs. "These are those paintings where the eyes follow you," Morgan said softly. "So creepy."

They peeked in the ballroom, where staff were busy preparing for a wedding. The tall walls were decorated to look like they were built out of small boulders, making the room look like an ancient castle dining hall even though it had been recently built. They climbed a narrow staircase on the way to their room. The handrail was polished brass, the walls were covered in pink wallpaper with damask shapes and there were more portraits hanging, along with pictures of people riding horses across open fields.

"I am turning into a softy being here," Morgan said. "All of this looks so romantic and pretty."

Jake placed his hand on her lower back. "Ireland does that to people. It's an ancient, magical place."

"Really, do you believe in magic Jake?"

"Course I do," he smiled his warm smile and bent to kiss her. "There's all sorts of magic here, y'know."

They spent the weekend at the hotel, enjoying the stone lined walls in their room, and lazy mornings in the four poster bed. They ate decadent, expensive food, and Morgan discovered that in small amounts, she rather liked blood pudding in her Caesar salad.

"Eating that stuff makes me feel like a badass," she said as they set out for the walking path. She used her right hand to lift her left arm and moved it around as they started their walk, then adjusted the sling so she could keep it comfortable.

"How's it feeling?" Jake asked, nodding at her arm.

"It's not," she said. "It doesn't seem to be recovering much even with all that killer physiotherapy I did back home."

"Give it a bit more time," he said throwing his arm casually over her shoulder.

"Yeah, about that. How much time do we have?" she said. "I mean, I know we are cooling our heels here, but I'm not sure how much more relaxing I can handle."

"We need to be ready to be over on the continent as soon as possible. But we can wait until you are better. A few more weeks, a couple of months. Whatever."

"I don't know if I can wait that long," she grunted.

"That's why we are hiking hard today. Gotta get that soft body of yours back in shape."

"I'm not out of shape!"

"No? Prove it then. Keep up and I'll race you to the first marker!"

They sprinted down the path. He shortened his pace to match her for 500 metres or so, and then took off like a rocket. Morgan continued to run at her usual speed, but before long her arm started throbbing, and she slowed her pace. She stopped as the pain became unbearable, and removed her arm from the sling to stretch it out.

Jake circled back. He looked at Morgan's pinched face and slipped his hand around her waist, guiding her back to the comfort of the castle.

"Let's try it again," she said later.

"What?"

"Running. I'll keep the arm out of the sling and see how it goes."

"There's a forest park off the grounds here, with lots of trails. How about a walk?"

"I've been walking for weeks. I need to run."

"You work that arm too hard, and it may never come back. When you see my physiotherapist the week after next there'll be a lot more answers."

"Can we go sooner? I'm ready and this waiting is killing me." She looked at him and reached up on tiptoe to pull him in for a kiss.

"Fine," he said. "I will make a call, but best you be prepared. I think this therapy is going to hurt."

The next day they drove west toward Dundalk, and near the boundary to the town Jake turned to an old estate that had been extensively renovated. What looked like a farm operation from the road was a perfect front for the rehabilitation services offered to injured police, military, and the occasional spy. Morgan's therapy was going to begin in earnest.

CHAPTER 21

"It's a good thing I like you, or I'd have to hit you," Morgan said, rubbing her arm at the end of her second session with Rebecca. "That hurts like hell."

The petite physiotherapist looked at her. "I see this all the time, honey. Someone gets surgery and the doctor says great, it all looks fine. They want you to rest so your stitches and all that stay together, and then the physio you start with is gentle. With your injury where the blood had no where to go and flooded all that tissue in your forearm, you've got a much bigger problem."

Rebecca was not a "just out of school" physiotherapist like the one that Morgan consulted in Canada. She was close to Morgan's age, early 40s, and tough as hell. Morgan liked her immensely, even if the therapy was excruciating.

"Congrats on yer man, by the way," Rebecca said as she returned the small hand weights to their stand. "I'm impressed as hell that someone slowed that Jake down long enough to get him to notice. He is one handsome, sweet bloke."

"Thanks, I understand you've put him back together a few times."

"Oh yes. I can't for the life of me understand why men his age still play rugby, but there he was the first time I met him. Wham, crash, thumping around the pitch like a bunch of young men. Another time with ribs so painful he couldn't sit up straight."

"She thinks you get hurt playing rugby," Morgan laughed as she got in the car after her session ended. Having a laugh took her mind off the screaming agony in her arm.

"I did! The first time I saw her I'd been playing in the rain and ended up with a pulled hamstring and a broken wrist."

"Hmm. You are just full of surprises, Jake. Here I was thinking you were lying to cover up an injury on a mission someplace."

"Well, that was the case the second time when I had a rib problem. Some of this stuff you can't even make up," he smiled back at her.

Therapy on her arm was the most intense physical pain Morgan had ever encountered. "I should've had kids. At least with babies is you know that the pain of delivery goes away, and then you have a baby to cuddle. This is really feckin' dragged out," she said, testing out her Irish cuss words.

Rebecca laughed at Morgan's attempt with the word feckin'. "It's only been two weeks," she said helpfully.

"It's not getting much better though, is it?"

"No," the physiotherapist agreed. "It's not. I think we should try something else."

"What's that?"

"You need to go see a doc over in London. It's expensive treatment, but in the last couple of years they've made good advances with it. They basically remove some of your blood, create a super cocktail with it, and then put it back in ye."

"Sounds a bit hocus pocus," Morgan said warily.

"It's summertime in London. You'll enjoy the break from me, and get away from this wretched rain while you enjoy some cocktail magic. Then come back, and we'll jump right back in."

Morgan was sure there was some hocus pocus involved in the London Cocktail, though she never actually witnessed any. Tissue that had felt like rubber from the outside of her arm actually changed, and when Morgan poked her finger into the fleshy part of her forearm, she could see white around her finger, and then when she pulled her finger out of the muscle, the skin became pink again.

Rebecca the Wicked, as Morgan started to call her, was thrilled when Morgan returned to Ireland. "Oh my God," she said. "It worked!" Her pixie cut hair bobbed and her blue eyes sparkled as she stroked Morgan's arm. "I wasn't totally sure, y'know. But look at this arm, it's alive! This is marvellous indeed."

The next four weeks were gruelling, and Morgan worked harder than ever to regain the proper use of her arm. To work her other muscles and stop from getting bored, she also did some farm chores. She forked hay for the two old horses in the stable, and brushed them for hours. When her arm throbbed and she was trying not to cry in front of Rebecca, she'd go into the barn and curse. She yowled and hollered just like the angry, tortured, soul she was. She sipped out of her Scotch flask and then yelled a little more, until the day Clint, a retired stallion, walked up to her and leaned his head over her good shoulder like he was giving her a hug.

It was several more weeks of therapy before Morgan's arm started functioning under its own free will, but eventually she could raise it up to shoulder height as if nothing had happened, although she still couldn't reach high enough to hold the blow dryer up there.

"Good," Jake said, grinning while she forked hay into Clint's stall. "We can get in and out of Ukraine then. What do you think?"

"Alright," Morgan said, finishing her work in the stall. "When do we go?"

"Are you sure that arm of yours is holding up okay?"

"Yeah, and now that I've learned to shoot almost as well with my left hand, I'm double the trouble I was before."

Jake laughed. She was used to his laugh by now, and their life in Ireland. It had been a good season of rest, being tourists, sharing long lazy days and cozy steamy nights. But, despite the agony of her rehabilitation sessions, she was itching to get back into the field, and so was Jake.

The following day, she and Jake sat across the table from Director Steeves, who'd come to check on them from London.

"Are you getting itchy feet yet, Winfeld?" he asked.

"Yes sir, and if I don't get back to work soon all these scones I'm eating will be permanently attached to my butt."

"This is mostly a recce mission, one of your favourites." He said with a wink to Morgan. "Just keep yourselves a low profile and try not to disappear while you are there."

After the director left, Jake looked at Morgan. "Any nightmares lately?"

"No, not at all...unusual actually."

"Maybe you've broken the routine by getting shot," Jake suggested helpfully.

"Yeah, or it's some kind of magical Irish spell you're using."

"Well, I do my best," he said, sipping at his coffee.

"Yeah, or it broke my radar. I guess we'll wait and see," she said, distractedly, flipping through the briefing notes on her mobile. "Jake, how much of this could we be doing online, d'you think?"

"A lot, but we can't always get access established without somehow going in there first. Once we meet with Trawler in person, it'll unfold quick enough."

"Trawler? Our contact's name is Trawler?"

"I don't imagine that's his real name," Jake laughed.

They were travelling light, posing as tourists on a four day excursion to historic Kiev. They would be met by a driver at the airport, and taken to a three star hotel near downtown.

"We must have made someone mad to get stuck in this place," Morgan said as they stepped into the hotel elevator. The crate shook as it left the lobby and shuddered unsteadily as it ascended to the fifth floor.

"We're meeting Trawler in the hotel bar in 20 minutes. Just enough time to freshen up and get a view of the city." Jake approached the window and looked out into a smog filled sky, though the view of the street below was clear. He pulled out a tablet, a gift from the director so they weren't carting laptops and taking up so much space in their bags, and sent off an encrypted message to Stan to let him know they'd arrived.

"That shower is really a letdown," Morgan said as she finished her tour of their room. "You're going to have a time getting your head under it."

They had developed a rule for work, and her tone of conversation let Jake know she had already adjusted and was primed for the job. She pulled a scarf from the recesses of her pack and wrapped it around her neck a couple of times for a more touristy bohemian look to her otherwise simple white t-shirt, jeans, and dark brown leather jacket.

They approached the hotel bar quietly, registering the noise from the televisions hanging around the edges as the patrons sat engrossed watching soccer. All except one man, seated at a tall table, a beer in front of him that he had yet to touch. He was trim and 50-ish with a tidy beard that almost hid a deep scar travelling from the corner of his drooping mouth to the bottom of his left ear. He looks like Val Kilmer, Morgan thought, as she noted the small sharp eyes, and flat visage. Trawler, or Val as she would always think of him, nodded to her and Jake, and indicated the chairs at the table.

"Welcome to Kiev," he said in his accented English. "I trust your flight was okay."

"Very okay," Jake said. "Thank you for the pick up at the airport."

"Best way to greet new friends is to make sure they get to the hotel, and have everything they need." Trawler had arranged for a limo ride, complete with a driver, and some gifts in the trunk. Jake and Morgan each had two sidearms and enough accessories to get them through their visit.

"Let's take a walk around the neighbourhood," Trawler said in a friendly tone as he drained his beer. "I'll show you what's nearby."

Just like any tour guide, Trawler showed them the cafés and restaurants he recommended, and he handed them a map that highlighted the tourist attractions, including the historic gilded Orthodox church nearby.

"Here," he jabbed the map with his pen, making his cigarette bounce between his lips at the same time, "is a place you should see. It's a shop with some good deals on costumes that are traditional. You know, red stitching and wood dolls and stuff you can buy to take back home for your souvenirs."

They knew that across the street from this shop was an office of great interest to them.

"Great, just what I want to do is go shopping," Jake said sarcastically as he eased into character. "Can I have a couple of your smokes until I get some at the shops?"

"Sure," Trawler said, handing Jake the package with a lighter tucked inside and the access code for the keyless entry written on one of the cigarettes. "Anything else you need, you just let me know. And stay off these streets at night. Not a very nice neighbourhood after dark."

The next morning started bright and clear. There were clouds on the horizon, and pigeons scattered outside the hotel as Morgan and Jake headed to a nearby café for breakfast. They pointed to the pictures on the plastic coated menu, laughing with their waitress who thought them silly Irish people for coming somewhere like this when they didn't speak the language at all.

Not wanting to arouse suspicion, they spread a new map on the table once the dishes were cleared away, used Google translate on their phone to talk to the waitress, and asked her for a place to buy souvenirs. She pointed out the window gesturing and, when she realized how clueless her customers were, she pointed to the map at the same store Trawler had indicated the day before.

The souvenir store was filled with handmade work, including peasant style blouses with colourful embroidery, small figurines of the local churches, and wooden nesting dolls. They made a big deal out of looking and picking things up, while keeping an eye on the window at the building across the street. Morgan paid for her purchases and joined Jake on the street where he was busy lighting a cigarette.

"Smoking already?"

"It's a helpful way to stand outside and watch," he said. Then he smiled leaned in and kissed her on the side of the neck.

"I just spent one hundred euros and all along you could have just stood out here and smoked?" she whispered as she smiled along with him. His kisses sent tingles through her and she didn't mind sharing a few to make passersby look away awkwardly and not register anything about the visitors.

"There's a lot of activity over there," he said cocking his head toward the building across the street. It was a three-storey office building that was past its prime twenty years ago. The front windows were dirty, and the brickwork was falling apart.

Morgan grabbed her phone and put one earpiece in, as though she were listening to directions in one ear and her husband in the other. She opened her shopping to allow him to have a look at what she'd bought, while her device scanned for voices across the way. All she heard was static.

"Ach, my mother. She'll kill me if we don't take her a present," he said. "Here, hold my smoke."

Jake went back into the store, and Morgan looked across the street. It seemed there was even more action out the back than in front. When Jake returned without a gift, she said, "We can always come back tomorrow honey. You don't have to decide right away."

They pretended to be tourists that day, joining a bus tour with an English guide so they could fit in and get a sense of where they were.

There were a lot of dark alleys and corners on the drive back to their hotel, along with red blinking lights of security cameras.

"We don't have a lot to go on," Jake said. "Let's check and see if the bugs we left at the store have picked anything up."

They uploaded the recordings for Stan to have translated, but there wasn't much to work with. The traffic at the store had been light, and there was plenty of interference on the recording.

They had a meal in the hotel bar that night, waiting for dark so they could slip out and go back around the corner.

"I'm going out to grab a smoke. Want to join me?"

"Sure," Morgan said. "We can take a stroll and walk off some of that supper."

Their supper had been heavy, and she did really need a walk but not as badly as they needed some information. As they headed for the door, a hotel clerk stopped them.

"Are you going out for the evening? Do you like a taxi?" His English wasn't great, but his intentions were.

"It's okay," Jake said holding up a cigarette. "Just popping out for a smoke."

"This neighbourhood is not good," the young man said. "Smoke on your balcony is safe. Too many not nice people here at night."

"Oh, thank you for telling us," said Morgan. "We were fine here today, and wanted to see the night life."

The man leaned to them conspiratorially. "Lots of people around at night with no love in their hearts."

"What kind of people?" Morgan said, leaning toward him.

"Russians, Ukrainians, but not friend." He placed his arm behind Morgan's shoulders to encourage her to take the elevator. "Not friendly at night."

"Mate, we're okay," Jake said. "Thanks. We'll take a taxi ride if we decide to go somewhere."

He took Morgan's hand and led her to the street, where he lit a smoke and surveyed their surroundings. Cars with two and three passengers were passing the hotel, with curious looks at the foreigners. Music blasted loud and crude from several of the cars.

"Okay, let's go grab some gear and then we will leave out the back," Jake said, putting his cigarette into the ashtray and smashing it.

They moved quickly once back outside, and set up watch with a good view of the rear of the ugly office building. The dark felt like a welcome blanket to Morgan. She let it envelope her, and tucked herself into the shrubs as far as she could. There were no cameras on this side street that they could see, and the traffic was lighter. When she caught the scent of a European cigarette, she and Jake stood motionless, but the smoker passed them by without noticing they were lurking in the shadows.

They stayed there all night, standing pressed into the bushes, alternating with sitting on their heels to stay awake and avoid getting stiff. There was a steady string of cars in and out of the battered parking lot. These were mostly arrivals between 10 p.m. and midnight, followed by departures between 4 and 6 a.m.

Vehicle occupants couldn't be seen because of the dark, but they did notice that there was no one coming to the office on foot or bicycle. That meant that at least some of these folks were being paid enough to buy a car. Jake tried the code that Trawler had given him for the keyless entry, but it didn't open the door. They hung around for another 30 minutes, watching to make sure their cover wasn't blown and seeing some of the early morning shift arrive, before heading back to their hotel room.

"Trawler, any luck on getting me that job?' Jake said into the phone. "Yeah, I know my Serbian is a bit rusty, but I need to have a look around and I couldn't get in. Thanks."

He turned to Morgan. "I'm going to work tonight as an office cleaner. You okay here on your own?"

"Of course," she said. "But be careful. All this clandestine activity and no signals picked up from the inside of that place is giving me the heebie jeebies."

"Spider tingling?"

"Yeah," she said. "Spidy senses tingling."

CHAPTER 22

Jake returned to the hotel following his cleaning shift tired and ready for a shower. Trawler's contact had worked him hard vacuuming stairwells, emptying bins, and then dusting the light fixtures but the employees had ignored him thinking he was a Serbian immigrant and wanting little to do with him. He was going to tell Morgan that he had heard plenty of conversations in several languages, and the place was definitely what they had hoped it was.

He opened the hotel room door quietly, expecting to find Morgan sleeping. Instead, he saw her tied to a chair, her hair tousled, and blood on her lip. That was all he registered before he was hit from behind, and he fell to all fours on the short gray hotel carpet. He heard a grunt from behind him as whoever hit him lifted the wood block to strike him again, and quickly rolled to the side while kicking the attacker's legs from under him and knocking him into the bed.

"Stop!" someone yelled, "Or I will shoot her, right here."

Jake looked over to see a woman, ex-military type, with a gun pointed at Morgan. He felt a kick to his ribs as the attacker moved clear of Jake's long reach.

"Who are you?" Jake growled.

"The questions will come from me," the woman with the gun said, pointing it at Jake's chest. "Now, who are you?"

"Are we going to play that game?" Jake said standing up, huge within the room even in his navy coloured janitor's coveralls.

"You don't belong here," the attacker said in heavily accented English. "And yet you are pushing your way around, and our boss wants to know who you are. You left out the back of this hotel and were gone all night two nights ago, and then last night you were gone again. What kind of shit are you pulling here?"

"I told them we were here on holiday," Morgan said through gritted teeth.

"Shut up," the woman said. Her hand started to shake from the weight of the revolver or from holding her arm extended. Morgan couldn't be sure, but the weakness was noted. Morgan's handcuffs were tight on her wrists, and she could not see the thug that was with this woman, which meant he had to be behind Morgan and off to one side slightly.

She looked directly at Jake and blinked one time, like she had done in the airport when they first met. She stood suddenly, using the top of her head to hit the woman under the chin and sending her reeling. The thug gasped, cursing something that sounded Russian, and fumbled to catch the woman as Jake grabbed his gun from the nightstand drawer.

Pfft, pfft. Two rounds through the silencer as the man and woman collapsed on the floor, blood pooling onto the industrial carpeting beneath them.

Jake searched their pockets for a key and identification and came up empty handed. "We need you out of those cuffs and out of here," he clipped. "Where the hell's the key?"

"I don't know," said Morgan, "but we better do it fast before their backup arrives." She caught her breath as Jake stood and stepped close to her. She shook her head as if to say, "what are you doing?"

Pfft. Another round into the guy who had started to stir. Jake found the key in the dead man's shoe and released Morgan. She quickly pulled clothes over her pyjamas, and shoved a hat over her messy hair. She had been sound asleep when the intruders snuck into her room.

There was no one in the hall, and they didn't want to risk the elevator so headed for the emergency stairs. The stairs were locked.

"We can't take the elevator. Too risky," she whispered. "Where to?"

They were on the top floor of the hotel, but there was no obvious entrance to the roof. "Check the utility room, where the ice machine is," Jake said indicating the small loud room down the hall. "Hurry, the elevator is moving."

They sprinted down the hall. They knew how to move without thudding their feet, and they made hardly a sound. Morgan edged open a staff access door just beyond the ice and pop machine, and then entered a small galley kitchen, where noises told them staff were preparing breakfast for the guests on this floor. A young woman in a chef's coat and ridiculous looking hat looked at Morgan and Jake's dishevelled states, quickly putting together what was going on.

"Go." She said pointing to the back stairs. "Hurry."

They scurried through the back door down the employee stairs moving like a pair of fugitives. When they reached the main floor, they stopped long enough to stow their revolvers at their backs, and to secure their back packs snugly. Jake cracked open the door slightly and could see the young concierge at his post.

"Morning," Jake greeted him as if there was no chaos on the top floor. "We're checking out."

"It's very early sir. Too early for good taxi. Can I help you?" the man suddenly looked like a boy. He was perhaps 19.

"We'll manage," Jake said. "And you were right about this neighbourhood at night. It is very dangerous."

"Yes sir. I know. And right now, there are Russians looking for you."

Jake pressed a hundred-euro bill into the boy's hand. "I am sorry, but there is a mess up in our room."

Morgan pulled the young man in for a hug and said into his ear, "There are people outside. We need to get out of here without being seen."

The boy paused only for a moment as he weighed out his options. "The hotel owns a small bus in the parking lot behind hotel. The keys are here and you could easily steal them from me."

"Thank you," Morgan said. She startled the boy as she pulled him down to her height and kissed him on both cheeks.

"We don't like the Russians being bossy," he whispered. "God save Ukraine."

CHAPTER 23

"I feel like we are playing a scene out of the Cold War," Jake said as they made their way to the hotel bus. There was a big decal on the six-passenger van door, announcing the name of the hotel.

"Let's head to the Canadian embassy and see if we can work some diplomatic way out of here. 'Cause there is no way we are going to be sneaky in this van," Jake suggested.

"I don't know if we want to bring attention to them," said Morgan. "They have a great relationship with the Ukraine government."

"How about the Americans?"

Morgan was already checking her phone for directions. "Turn left up there, we're about 15 minutes away. Give me your phone."

"What?"

"Trade me phones. I'll call Trawler."

"He could be part of our problem. I don't know."

"Well, right now, he's our best option. We can't go to the airport or they will be looking for us, and we're without paperwork to cross a border plus driving in this thing I feel like we have a big target on our butts."

"Oh shit," Jake said, drawing up to the middle of the street their GPS had brought them too. The American embassy was there, once, but the walls lay in pieces, the fence was in disarray, and the grounds were scarred black and brown.

"Feck! Let's hope Trawler answers." Morgan said. She tapped his name on the screen.

"Yes," he answered in a sleepy voice.

"Sorry to wake you Trawler, but we could use your help. We are looking for safety and came to the US embassy."

"Oh, that was bombed out last year. Why you don't go to the Canadians?"

"Because they may not have the resources there to help us Trawler. They are an administrative staff."

"Okay." Trawler replied. "Where are you? I come to you?"

"We are near the American embassy. Probably being followed, and we are in a van with the hotel painted all over it."

"Pretend to go to the Canadian embassy. Give them something to think about," Trawler said. "I will find you."

"I do not like being in this van at all," Jake said. Out of the corner of his eye he caught movement. "Shit, a drone. Get down so they can't tell we are both in here."

Morgan did as she was told, trying to bring up directions for the Canadian embassy. "Jake, it's a 30-minute drive from here."

"We need to ditch the van," Jake said. He did a quick right turn into a shopping complex that had a small parking structure attached to it. He headed for the ramp. "Hold on," he said. "We're going in."

Once inside, the cement was effective at slowing the drone, but it wouldn't be long before the police showed up.

CHAPTER 24

"I have an idea," Morgan said, "But you're going to have to trust me."

"You know I trust you."

They were hunkered down in a corner of the parking structure, their backpacks providing a padded layer to lean on between them and the cold concrete.

"The shops here are open. I'm going to go into that one there at the end and grab us some gear. You stay here with our stuff."

"Are you out of your mind? That drone can't be far, the GPS from the van is probably screaming at the police. What do we need?"

"We need you out of your janitor's coveralls."

"I thought these made me look cute," he said, but the smile didn't make it to his eyes.

"The pants are too short and you look like an escaped criminal with all that stubble on your face."

She stuck to the shadows, and went into the first store, a place with men's work clothes hanging in the window. She quickly selected two Carhartt jackets off the rack, working gloves, and black toques. She hoped she was reading the tags correctly as she selected jeans and a belt for Jake. Now they could move about the city a little less obviously.

Jake changed in the dark corner of the parkade, just as they heard sirens on the main road. The sleeves on his jacket were a bit short, but otherwise things were a good fit.

"I usually get my jackets off the rack for tall guys," he said, cocking an eyebrow at Morgan.

She replied by sticking her tongue out at him.

They made their way to the far edge of the parkade just as the police came up the ramp. At the back door, Jake motioned to Morgan that the way was clear, and they snuck out of the parkade in search of Trawler.

Morgan placed a call to Stan to give him an update. "I wondered when you would finally pick up the phone," he said. "I've been waiting for more than an hour."

"Yeah, we've been really busy."

"Look, can you get to a metro station? Once you are on a train, it's tougher for them to find you, though you need to be careful...the stations are littered with cameras. When you get to the north end of Line 2 – it shows as blue on their transit maps – Trawler can pick you up."

"Stan, we were spotted by a drone. I can't see it now, but there was one that followed the van to the parkade."

"That was me," Stan said. "Don't worry."

Morgan let out a long slow breath of relief that the drone was theirs. "Lucky break," she said to Jake. She messaged Trawler to meet them at the end of the train line.

They made their way out of Ukraine driving a Volvo that just barely accommodated Jake's frame. The paperwork and passports they carried identified them as Irish and Trawler had also given them a suitcase each of clothes that didn't belong to them so they could cross the border into Poland. They drove all night, pulling into the airport in Warsaw exhausted, and took the first plane they could get to London.

CHAPTER 25

"You look like shit, both of you," the Director said as a greeting outside the café. He took a drag from an e-cigarette before waving Jake and Morgan through the door ahead of him. Morgan looked at him closely as she passed in front. His face was well-lined, heavily accented by a sergeant major's distinctive style moustache. They were meeting at a small café near Heathrow Airport, and she took a seat in the garden while Jake went to the counter to place their order. The place was right next to a busy street, and cars honked as though their fury would help get traffic moving. Morgan watched the four lanes of chaos until the director and Jake took their seats. She wearily took a sip of her cappuccino.

"Yeah, well we all know that the days of sneaking into other countries is pretty much over, sir. It's just about impossible to move around without someone knowing you're there." Jake said.

"I agree. We're certainly doing a lot more by leveraging tech, but if you hadn't been able to get into that office and place those bugs or get us some of those files, we wouldn't know what we know."

"Surely, they have blocked your access since they obviously knew what we were up to," Morgan said.

"They're working on it, but no, they've not kicked us out yet and the bugs are still picking up more than we imagined possible. That place is a hotbed of messages and espionage, the trouble will be deciphering what's real and what's being said for our benefit."

"So, what's next?" Jake asked, looking at the director. His face was taught and his eyes were hard.

"You two need some downtime. Take a couple of week's holiday and I'll get back to you. Your recce was a great success, and Morgan, you've tested your arm and things are working. So, go visit Cornwall or something. I hear that it's beautiful there this time of year."

"Sir, I'm not in any need of a holiday. As you know, we came off a very long break just before this," Morgan said politely.

"Don't worry Morgan, I have it on good authority that you'll find yourself some kind of trouble. There's a new agency car at the office that you can take. It's got lots of legroom and a motor that won't quit. Just don't break it, or I'll have to hunt you both down and kill you, alright?"

CHAPTER 26

It wasn't just any kind of agency car the director had loaned them. Jake gave a low whistle when he first looked it over. It was an Aston Martin, made to look like the 2003 roadster that had been created as a touring car for the American market, but this one had a metal top as required by the agency – there were no convertibles allowed, naturally. There were a few modifications done to the V-12 6-cylinder engine to put it in top shape. As an added bonus, the director had told them sternly, it was bullet proof and had a top speed of about 190 miles per hour, which was not advisable on the country roads they would be on, and not authorized either.

"If I was a bit shorter, I'd think I was James Bond," Jake said as ran his hand across the bonnet.

"Which Bond would you be?" Morgan asked as she stowed her gear in the trunk. "Connery? Craig? Moore? Dalton? Brosnan? I can't remember the names of the others."

"I'm impressed you know that many of them; I'm not sure I can. I think I'd mix together Connery and Brosnan for charm and sex appeal, and add a dash of Craig for grit and tenacity. Not too much Craig of course...he is such an angry person."

"Oh my God," Morgan said, fluttering her lashes and patting her chest dramatically, "this is the realization of a lifelong dream. I'm going on an adventure with James Bond."

"Yes, well, be careful," he said clearing his throat nervously, "You know what happens to Bond women..."

"Yeah, they always end up dead," Morgan said seriously, and then to lighten the mood she added, "So I should drive first. That way I at least have a chance to play with this beauty before I get shot, blown up, or drowned."

She drove for the first hour and opened the engine up. The car clung to the road on tight corners, and responded to even the smallest changes on the throttle. And, it was damned fast.

Late that day, Jake pulled to the side on the main street of Tintagel, on the coast of Cornwall. Morgan stepped from the car slowly, stretching her legs while taking in the view.

"This place is charming," she said. "And it smells good." She breathed deeply, "It...it smells like the sea."

"Have you been here before?"

"No, but I love it already."

"Well, wait until we get to the castle."

Tintagel was the place of legend, perched as it was along the southwest corner of Britain. It was reportedly the birthplace of King Arthur, and had been occupied by the Romans over long periods. The people who lived there year round had to be the tough variety, given the storms and cold that rolled off the ocean.

Morgan and Jake were staying at the very charming King Arthur's Arms Inn, a four star bed and breakfast. As they settled into their room, Morgan laid back on the bed for a moment, catching the breeze floating in through the open window. She closed her eyes and listened while Jake put a couple of bottles of cola in the fridge and a bottle of Scotch – a gift from the director, on the desk. He sat down next to her on the bed, and placed his warm hand on her stomach. "I can feel the heat of your hand through my shirt," she said, sleepily.

"Yeah, well, this James Bond guy is hot," he said. He leaned over and kissed her deeply. Pulling away only a little he whispered into her ear, "Do you want to nap?"

"Not at all," she replied, pulling him close. "I have James Bond here in my bed, and you know what happens when a woman gets this close to James Bond, don't you?"

"No, I haven't seen the movies in ages," he whispered back, a smile easing its way onto his tanned face.

"She kisses him, and then in the next scene they are twisted in the sheets, all sweaty."

He slid his hand underneath her t-shirt. "Let's see if we can make a better movie than that, shall we?"

CHAPTER 27

The following day, Morgan and Jake strolled around the castle, and climbed hundreds of stairs among the rocks.

"Imagine living somewhere like this," Jake said. "Talk about being exposed. You could see your enemies coming from the sea, but once they get close in these rocks you wouldn't know they were right on top of you."

"I'd be more worried about the ones on the land," Morgan said. "I was reading some information that said Arthur moved here from Camelot to be more secure. They never figured out where exactly Camelot was."

"I think the best guess was somewhere in Wales. We can head there after we wear out this place if you like."

"Good idea. We can do some investigating without having to worry about world peace for a bit."

"Ha," Jake snorted, pulling her close. "These old stories are about world peace, too. The Celts being pushed west from Britain by the Anglo-Saxons is all mixed with Arthurian legends about fighting between the lot of them. The site they believe could have been Camelot is likely a Roman fortress built after Arthur left. All of them trying to create a place where they could live in peace and harmony."

"What about the Lady of the Lake and all that? Do you know any of that story?"

"Not much. There are theories that the lake of Avalon was here somewhere, or off the coast, or even in continental Europe, though I personally think the latter is shite. Travelling that far repeatedly in those days meant you had to be kitted out like a Saxon battle unit, or the Roman army. I kind of like the version that says it was in Ireland, though, land of magical tales and stuff. But who knows? Most legends have a sprinkling of truth to them, but there's a lot you have to take on faith."

CHAPTER 28

They spent four days exploring Tintagel, being decadent and staying in bed late, and being tourists zipping around in the car during the day, visiting all the pubs and tourist spots in the area. Jake looked at Morgan over breakfast one morning, and said "Your hair is getting long. It's curling and playful looking."

"Yours is growing out too," she said. "You don't look quite so military when it hangs over your forehead like that. Do you suppose that's what the director is hoping for?"

"Oh probably," he smiled. "And just because we know he's watching, I am going to stuff myself with eggs and blood pudding this morning."

"What do you say to driving up to Wales afterward? I have roots up there somewhere."

"Sure," he said.

When they arrived in Rhyl on the coast of Wales late the next afternoon, the sky was dark and pregnant looking, ready to unleash a huge storm. The breeze was bitter.

"Wow, this place looks beautifully dark and creepy," Morgan said. "Look at the cloud."

Jake grunted his agreement, then added, "Tell me again why you are suddenly fascinated with this part of your family tree?"

"I've always been fascinated with it. And since we are on a forced vacation, I went digging around in my mom's family tree where there are a couple of loose ends. Rhyl is one of them."

Jake shook his head. "You just never relax, do ye?"

She smiled at him impishly. "Relax? For what? Let's stop at the information centre there, and see what we can find."

There were several churches and graveyards in the small town. Morgan wanted to check the grave markers and see if her ancestor was there.

"When my mom was a girl, the story was that she was the daughter of a man from Rhyl who disappeared right after he married my grandmother. The rumour was that he was a bigamist, but despite that there was no easy way out of it. My grandmother had to work three jobs to afford the divorce. When my mother told me the story, I was suspicious. I mean, why would you have to pay for a divorce if the marriage wasn't legal?"

"What'd you find out?"

"Just dead ends. Mom had his service number because this was during World War Two and it was recorded on her birth certificate, but it turned out to be one of those numbers with no records attached to it. We found all kinds of records of people who were in his army unit, but nothing else. Plenty of records were kept in London in those days but there were also loads of them that are missing."

"Sounds like a good mystery for an agent on vacation," Jake said. He put his warm hand on her thigh as he drove, and his warmth tingled right through to her insides. They pulled up to the parish office the bright young clerk at the information centre had recommended.

"That name yer searchin' for is pretty common around here," the parish clerk said. "Let me fetch Father William, he's been here the longest." The women left her desk efficiently, and smoothed stray long strands of curly brown hair as she crossed the room to the hall.

The Father was an elderly man. His eyes were small and dark brown, framed by silver eyebrows that stuck out all angles over the top of his large tortoiseshell glasses. He carried himself like a young man, with his shoulders and back straight and a smile ready to greet them. He looked like a non-traditional priest though, Morgan thought, taking in his cigarette smoke stained fingers, and a white collared shirt and black blazer over top of worn corduroy pants. His black shoes were shiny and well looked after.

"Hallo folks. How can I help you? I understand you're looking for someone who's long dead?"

"Well I assume he is Father, since he married my grandmother during World War Two. I have only a few details. When my mother was researching her family tree she tried to find him, but no luck I'm afraid."

"And is your mother still alive?"

"No, I'm sorry to say she's not."

"Well why do you need to know so bad? Most ghosts are best left alone, I find, except for the good Lord, of course." He smiled at her, and the lines around his mouth doubled like they do on old men who were handsome in their youth. He clasped his hands in front of him and leaned back on his heels, waiting for her to speak.

"There was a lot of mystery about it in my family, is all," Morgan said, willing the man to help. "And since we were here anyway, it seemed like a good idea to ask."

"What kind of mystery?"

"The official story was that he was a bigamist. Married my gran, got her pregnant immediately, and then disappeared to marry someone else, but apparently he had married a third woman a year before he married my gran. Funny thing was when I started to do my research I found lots of information online about marriages that ended in bigamy charges, like it was a trend or something."

"Oh aye, there you are then. In those days young people were scared of dying. Being in love made the war less frightening, y'know? You don't believe your gran's story?"

"Well, it just seems very convenient. She got divorced on account of the bigamist marriage, and then met a Canadian soldier who was stationed in England. After the war ended and all the paperwork was done, she and her daughter – my mum – emigrated to Canada."

"The daughter being a result of the marriage to the bigamist?"

"Yes."

"Hmm, and what's this fellow's name you say?"

"It was Davies. James Edward Davies, and he is supposed to have been born in Rhyl."

"You know that digging around in people's pasts gets a bit scary for the people who are alive sometimes, right?"

"What do you mean scary?" Jake interjected.

"Well, people sometimes don't like foreigners poking around in their business."

"Are you suggesting there's something we need to be worried about, Father?" Jake said.

"Oh aye, I am." He raised his eyebrows over the top of his glasses, the hairs going every which way leaving him with a comical look on his lined face.

Morgan's hair stood on her arms. She looked at Jake. Suddenly the family tree hunt was not as harmless as she had hoped.

"Those Davies' were a pretty big family hereabouts, and Jimmy was no trouble really, but the family. Well, that was another matter. They stayed in Rhyl because they couldn't move any further west, but they weren't from here originally. They came from Cornwall somewhere. Old money I think."

"Can we be sure that this was the same Davies family that he would have come from? I understand Davies is a pretty common name in Wales.

"Aye, but not so common in Rhyl. Come with me to the library and we'll go through the records. You can see for yourself." He led the way to the back of the office.

"Grace," he called to the secretary. "We have some work to do. Be a dear and make some tea, would you?"

"Of course, Father. Kettle's on already, so it won't be a minute."

The room was lined with bookshelves that rose to the vaulted ceiling. The library was academic, with great tomes lining the shelves, and a ladder on wheels to reach the highest of them.

"Mostly for show, although the ladies like to dust it," Father William said indicating the stacks of books. He waved them through to an area separated from the library by a partition of metal filing cabinets. There was a very modern computer and an equally modern looking clerk at work.

"This is Margaret," Father William said. "She is digitizing all our records, not just the parish, but the town as well. She gets paid by grant from the government so she mostly does what she is supposed to, but sometimes we can ask her for small favours in return for cookies or a bottle of Scotch. Isn't that right Margaret?"

Margaret looked up from her computer and smiled fondly at the old man. Her curly light red hair was neatly tied at the nape of her neck, and the fluorescent lights made her pale skin look translucent. "It's true I have been known to moonlight for cookies and Scotch, Father. What do you need today?"

"Me, nuthin'," the man said, putting a hand to his chest and adopting an innocent look. "But these two here, they are asking some questions about the Davies' and I think you may have some information."

"The Davies family," she said, pressing a few keys. "Family property up on Langford, not far from the water, on a farm. Nowadays the farm is smaller, but the big old house is still there. Looks like it is still owned by the same family."

"Can we have an address and directions?" Morgan said as Grace put a tea tray down on a nearby table.

"You may want some more details before you go trotting over there," Margaret said. "Here, let me project this onto that screen there, so you can have a look."

Margaret's equipment was impressive. She pushed a button on her computer and her screen was quickly projected onto a piece of glass suspended over an old oak table in the middle of the library. She read off some of the notes.

"The Davies' have lived in the area since about the 1910s, when they moved from Cornwall. They farmed, mostly, and have had several generations living in the mansion, as well as a couple of other houses that used to be part of the property. It's been subdivided, but the Davies' still own the bulk of it."

"We're looking for James Edward Davies, born in 1920," Morgan said. "I have a few other details about him, here." She handed her notebook to Margaret.

"He was known as Jimmy," Father William piped up, "if we're talking about the same fellow."

"You remember practically everyone who ever grew up in this parish, Father," Margaret said as she looked gently at the old man.

"This is interesting," Margaret said, quickly reading through the notes on the screen. "Newspaper stories, and one about a James Edward Davies going missing in 1975. Says that he was found wandering about in a field several days later, badly beaten and mumbling about knights and swords and things. They trotted him off to rest at Boddelwyddan."

"What's that?" Jake asked.

"It's a castle and tourist attraction now," Margaret said. "At one time it served as a hospital and respite home. It looks as though they locked him up for a bit."

"Can I visit his family if they are still in the area?" Morgan asked.

"It seems like you will have to, but remember what I said. The Davies' don't come to church anymore so we've lost touch, but the stories have had some holding power to them." Father William said. "Be prepared."

CHAPTER 29

The house had aged well and the grounds outside were beautifully looked after. Morgan took a moment to appreciate it all as she approached the front door. Out of the corner of her eye she could see a Rottweiler sniffing the air to see how dangerous the company was. He cocked his head before sitting and looking straight at her. From inside, she could hear the barking of another big dog.

Morgan felt the hair rising on her right arm as she tapped the brass door knocker on the oversized door. She drew back after knocking, just as the big door opened to reveal a thin, small woman, with dark curly hair, threaded with shots of grey. She was about Morgan's age.

"Yes," she said. "I thought you'd be by. Come in." Ms. Davies took Morgan's coat, and asked someone to bring in tea and scones.

"I knew you were coming," Ms. Davis said. "I thought you might be a day or two off yet. My skills must be slipping a bit."

"Skills?" Morgan asked. "What skills exactly?"

"Oh dear. You don't know yet, but it's part of why you're searching. The skills. I have them, but my grandad really had them. You're here to see if he's really your grandad, too, right?"

She doesn't beat around the bush, Morgan thought. "Well...yes. I want to see if he was the man who married my grandmother and then somehow skirted around a quick divorce."

"Yes, that's always been the official word hasn't it. Divorce. Bigamy. But Jimmy Davies was none of those things really. He was a loving, kind man with a very serious job to do. He was destined to die doing it." She looked off in the distance, and pursed her lips. "His job was to make sure our people had longevity. In order to do that, he had to make sure there were plenty of progeny to carry on the family name."

"What?"

"Children. Progeny. You. Me."

"I'm not following. Are you saying that Davies...tricked my grandmother into marrying him so that she would get pregnant?"

"Not really, he did love all the women in his life. He wanted to be close to your gran, and their daughter, but once the Canadian showed up, Grandad Davies didn't have a lot of options. I had the benefit of him being around when I was young and he trained me to use the sight although I never really had anything special to apply it to. There are others of us out there, cousins I like to call them but really they are half-siblings and so on. If you are anything like some of the family that never got any training you probably noticed some weird things about yourself. You can feel things, sensations, you have vivid, spectacular dreams."

"Well, y...yes. I guess." Morgan thought about her visions of her husband, and of Jake.

"Do you have children? That's the part about you I've been trying to see. I was hoping you were young enough to have children still if you don't have some already."

"No, no children." Morgan felt like she was stammering under Ms. Davies' inquiries.

"I'm so sorry," the other woman paused, and she clasped her hand to her heart. "It means you are the end of your line, and I had hoped that wasn't the case. But, you can nurture and grow this strength you have inherited and make the most of it."

"How? What? I...I actually haven't had any dreams or visions for months."

"You just need waking up, Morgan. You've had things to deal with and the dreams and feelings may have stopped, but we can kick start them again. Jimmy Davies came from a line we can trace from the princesses – some people called them witches – of Avalon." She stood and moved to a tall bookcase, drawing out a leather bound book, and opened it to show a family tree.

"Are you talking about King Arthur and the legends and all that?"

"Well yes, and no. There is a lot of the history of that time that's been lost, and the legends are pretty captivating. People in our family know what happened, but we protect the truth. Most research and fiction that's been created is just that – a lot of fiction. We do know that Arthur lived in the transition time when there was a huge decline in pagan worship, and the rise of Christianity. He was a pagan himself, and converted to Christianity for his wife, Guinevere. We have some incredible journals that have been passed through time from the princesses of Avalon. Arthur wasn't out to rule the world. He just needed to carve out enough of one to build a kingdom so his family and the people they looked after would have a peaceful place to live."

"Peace." Morgan said. "That's a theme that keeps coming up lately."

"Yes," Ms. Davies said. "Speaking of which, I had a vision of you in snow and bullets, and on a snow machine or something. Are you a peacekeeper?"

"You had a vision about me?" Morgan asked.

"Do you always ask questions to avoid giving answers?" Ms. Davies asked directly.

"Yes," Morgan said. "I do. And yes, I'm a peacekeeper of sorts."

They had a long talk, Ms. Davies and Morgan. They shared stories about nightmares, premonitions, and spidy senses.

"I never heard them called that," Ms. Davies laughed.

"What am I supposed to do with this power, exactly?" Morgan said.

"Protect it," Ms. Davies said. "And use it. For your entire life, you have to use what you have inherited to fight the fight. Create peace. Watch out, take precautions, because people will try and kill you for that power. They either want it and think they can take it from you, or they don't understand it and think you're a threat."

"You mean I probably shouldn't put all this family history on ancestry.com under my real name?"

"That and so much more," Ms. Davies said, with a high pitched infectious giggle. "You're practically the perfect spy in this day and age, because you can access information with what's in your head. Just observe, absorb, and be open to what's coming."

"I never said I was a spy."

"You didn't have to, but why else would you be crossing borders and sneaking around in foreign countries while a peacekeeper? That's just come in my vision now. I also see a delicious man with you."

Morgan sat quietly for a moment, letting it all sink in.

"So, I'm the last of my line and have no one to take this on after me."

"That's okay," Ms. Davies said gently. "I think your purpose is to do your job to the very best of your ability, and create peace. My purpose is to help you flourish and to make sure my kids do the same. And try not to get shot again, of course. The path ahead of you has many dangers, but I see you managing them as long as you don't do anything stupid. I can teach you to protect yourself better."

"Sneaking into other countries is getting harder, of course, although the technology gets more helpful all the time. I was toying with the idea of becoming a private investigator, but the idea of chasing wayward husbands isn't really that compelling. Besides, I love what I do."

"I'm sure you'll figure something out. In the meantime, I am here as a resource for you and if you visit during a school break you would be able to meet my kids. Three of them already have shown very high degrees of perception, and one I'm hoping is a late bloomer, but we shall see. They are all away at university."

When Morgan left, the outdoor Rottweiler was sleeping in the sinking sun outside the front door. He got up, stretched, and approached Morgan with his entire back end wagging.

"That's Gareth," Ms. Davies said. "And he likes you."

CHAPTER 30

By the time Morgan returned to the parish office, Jake and Father Williams were dozing in the library. A bottle of Scotch was open on the table between them. Margaret was still at work in her alcove.

Jake roused at the sound of Morgan's approach. "How'd it go?"

"I don't even know, and yet I know so much."

"Is he yer Grandpa?" Father Williams asked even though his eyes were still closed.

"Yes, he is."

"Well, well, well." Father Williams said. "So, you're understanding what that means, right? You've got big responsibilities."

"Do you know a lot about him? The family?" Morgan asked.

"Oh aye," he said with a wink. "Jimmy was family to me too. We're what you'd call cousins."

Margaret looked at Jake, "You are both welcome to stay here tonight. I'm sure you have more questions, and there are guest rooms in the loft."

"I'll be in touch Margaret. For now, I think I'd like to let this all sink in a bit, if it's all the same to you." Morgan said.

Morgan was tired when they arrived at the hotel, but her brain wouldn't shut up. "Do you want to walk along the beach?" Jake asked, his hand around her shoulders feeling the tension under her shirt.

"Yes, good idea. It's cold and that should bring me back to me senses."

He held her hand as they left the hotel and crossed the path toward the beach. The wind was chilly and they both pulled hoods up from their sweaters.

"It's not any colder than it was earlier," he smiled. "But you are trembling. Here, let's run a bit and warm you up."

They fell into an easy pace together, and ran for several minutes. Morgan knew this was a bit of torture for Jake, because his legs were longer than hers. She sped up, and he laughed, "No need to do that," he said.

"I'm doing it for me as much as you," she called back. She ran as fast as she could, flat out, and as she ran past the visions of the fiery plane crash, bombs exploding, and toward the shadow of a man who was her grandfather, or perhaps someone else. For once they weren't scary visions. They were frozen in time like a 3D photograph.

CHAPTER 31

They lay in bed the next morning, and Morgan stretched her body alongside Jake. He rolled onto his side, spooning her, and cupped a full breast in his hand, rubbing his thumb across her nipple.

"Mornin' beautiful," he said.

"Morning sexy," she said. "Gad, how I do enjoy waking up next to you. Maybe we ought to stay on holiday forever."

"Won't you be bored by next week though?" He kissed her neck, then slid his hand down her hip and along her thigh.

"Mmm," she said turning toward him, "If we keep waking up like this, I'm good for at least another couple of weeks."

Each afternoon that week, Jake headed off for a run and then went to visit Father Williams. Morgan spent those same hours with Ms. Davies learning how to focus on something, observe, and...coalesce, as Ms. Davies called it. It was strange and not as magical as Morgan expected.

"Concentrate!" Ms. Davies said in a shrill voice on the second afternoon.

"I am!" Morgan yelled. She was sitting on an overstuffed red leather chair in Ms. Davies' parlour, but she was barely perched on the edge of it as she concentrated on the wiggly images in her head. She'd told her mentor about the vision she glimpsed while running, and that there was an unknown man off in the distance. Ms. Davies was just as anxious as Morgan to learn who the lurker was.

"Harder!" Ms. Davies demanded.

"Fuck," Morgan sighed. "It's gone. The fog cleared, and poof, it's like a switch got turned off."

"What fog?" Helen asked.

"I keep seeing fog, and the strange man is...is there...in the fog. Maybe it's Jimmy, I don't know, but I can't quite see him and I don't know what he looks like."

"Two things, then," Helen offered. "First of all, stop the fog."

"Stop it? Why would I do that? The vision was there, inside the fog."

"You can work with it. Stop it from obscuring your vision. Create a little breeze, and clear it away so you are revealing what's hidden."

"A breeze?"

"Yes, just like you would manipulate a dream where you aren't quite asleep, you can move things around in that vision. Freeze frame, zoom, whatever you need."

"I've never tried to manipulate a dream. Can you do that?"

"Oh yes honey, of course."

"Okay," Morgan said. "Let's try and do it again."

After the third afternoon, Jake looked at her, "You look different," he said.

"I do?"

He laughed. "It's your hair," he said softly as he looked closer. "You've got white hair at your temples. You didn't have white hair before"

"It's all this thinking I'm doing," she said, peering into the mirror in the hotel bathroom, then, "Jeez, will you look at that. My hair is going white."

"Father Williams has been filling me in on a few things."

"I thought you two were drinking Scotch and telling lies to one another," she said.

"Well, there's some of that, sure. He's filled me in on the Davies family history, and more importantly he's told me how you fit into the lore of the family."

"Lore? Is that what you call it?" she wasn't laughing, but her eyes were crinkled, and the corners of her mouth were dancing.

"Maybe, but it's really just about me knowing how to keep an eye on you so you can do what you do best, and I can, you know...help out, maybe. Keep you safe."

"You don't have to keep an eye on me. I'm not learning anything magic or stuff that'll change what I normally do. I'll just...maybe...be able to see better."

"It's a little Star Wars and 'use the force' isn't it?" he asked gently, his hands brushing the white hair along both sides of her face.

"It might be," she said laughed nervously, "certainly it's become more than a Spiderman episode. I need to stop and pick up some hair dye."

He cupped her chin in his right hand, and rubbed his thumb along her jaw line. Then he kissed her eyebrows, and her temples.

Morgan's phone buzzed and she glanced at it over on the bureau. "Looks like it's time we returned to real life, Jake." She kissed him warmly on the lips, then walked over to the phone and tapped the answer button.

"Hello, Director. We were just talking about you," she said, holding the phone so Jake could hear, too.

"I know you are both enjoying a mystical magical vacation there, but we have a problem," the director said. "How quickly can you get to Sommerside?"

"Do you mean Summerside, on Prince Edward Island, in Canada?" Morgan asked.

"No, it's up near Liverpool, in England. About 10 years ago there was an industrial centre built there and there's some interesting goings on but we cannot pick up everything we need remotely. The local police are very well known and can't get anymore intel than they already have."

"We can leave here in about 20 minutes," Jake said. "It's only an hour's drive or so from here."

"Plan to leave at first light and in the meantime, I will get the details to you through Stan."

CHAPTER 32

Jake drove the Aston Martin through the fog and early morning light. The day was cool and humid, and the fog parted in front of them as though it was sneaking them off to work. He handled the car expertly along the twisting secondary highways to Liverpool.

They stopped at a café for breakfast and were quiet as they prepared to be back at work.

"You okay?" Morgan asked.

"Yeah, why do you ask?" Jake said looking up over the menu.

"You're quieter than usual this morning. What's on your mind?"

"Not much," he offered. "I spent some time here as a kid, and it always leaves me unsettled."

"What kind of time?"

"My mum was married to a guy from here. I ended up at a private school nearby for about four years and she died while I was on a school trip."

"That would have been tough. You never talk about your family." She put down her fork and looked at him, inviting him to continue.

He shrugged. "It's not stuff I like to talk about. She had a stroke when I was 15, and my stepfather pulled me out of school and shipped me back to Ireland to live with my paternal grandparents. I hardly knew them. My life was here, and then all of a sudden...it wasn't."

"What happened to your Dad?"

"He was a cop. He was killed when I was a lad, by an Englishman, if you can stand the irony."

"God, really? And then you end up living in England? Yikes."

"Yeah, like I said, not something I spend a lot of time talking about. I spent a lot of time in this region on school outings, and some unauthorized ones."

"What are you thinking we should do?"

"I think we should take a drive past my old school, and then we'll head out to get our research done."

An hour later they pulled up to the Liverpool Blue Coat School. The school was still closed at this time of the morning, and the old building stood tall and imposing against the dark sky and milling fog. Morgan read the inscription on a plaque beside the entry. *"Non Sibi Sed Omnibus.* What's that mean?"

"Not for oneself but for all," Jake translated.

"Sounds like another way of saying 'world peace,'" Morgan said softly.

"I thought it might be a good place to stop in case you want to practice your homework. See what you can see."

"I don't need to do it anywhere specific."

"Well, could you maybe try? See if you can see anything hereabouts or what's to come in the next day or so?"

"I can't force it like that Jake. What're you worried about?"

"There's been someone creeping around, and I was hoping you could figure out who it is before he either says hello or tries to kill us. He was wearing a school sweater of some kind when I saw him yesterday, but he was out of sync with the place."

"Where'd you see him? Here, in the fog you mean?" Morgan turned slowly around looking into the fog to see if there was anything hiding.

"No, it was perfectly clear when I saw him yesterday. He was lurking outside the library. Father William was none too pleased that he was there."

"I have seen...someone," Morgan said. "He has been in a few visions, with a long coat over a sweater but I can't see him well enough to know who he is. I thought perhaps it was Jimmy's ghost or something."

"I think it's someone more real than a ghost, judging from Father William's reaction," Jake said quietly.

They returned to the car in silence, and Morgan drove the rest of the way with a heavy foot on the gas pedal. There was no one following them, she made sure of that, but the notion of a man with his hands on his hips and a trench coat flapping in the wind revealing a crested sweater floated on the edge of her mind.

CHAPTER 33

They made their way to Vauxhall, on the edge of Liverpool, and Morgan looked at the mix of old buildings and newer construction as they drove through the industrial area and the seafront. Rounding a corner near a business with XSShipping in bright orange neon, Morgan looked over to a Land Rover poorly parked on her side of the road, and then snapped her head back to look at Jake.

"Every time I see a jeep, I'm ready to see one of those goons from Halifax," she said.

"What? Really?"

"Yes, I know it's weird, but that Land Rover gave me a start."

"Do you think it's something?"

"Not likely, but all of a sudden I want my gun."

Jake smiled. "Let's check in with Stan and see what other information he has collected."

Morgan stopped the end of the street, in a parking lot at the Liverpool Marina. She hit the speaker phone button on the dash, and gave Stan an update.

"Oh, by the way," Stan said. "We've learned the two goons, as you call them, were hired by the folks in Lunenburg. The one who survived the attack at Spray Harbour was part of the security team there to protect their drug operation and click farm from getting noticed. He'll be in jail for years since he was part of an international criminal group. The mayor of Lunenburg is extremely grateful to you both."

"Well, what do you know," Morgan said. A smile creased her face and lit up her eyes. "World peace, once again."

Jake reached up in a high five and she high fived him back.

"Let's go explore the boats on the marina, shall we?" Jake said. "I've always thought having a boat was a good idea, and now seems like a good time to do some investigating."

"Sure," Morgan agreed. "I'll just grab my backpack. I'll feel a little more secure with a gun at my side."

There was plenty to see at the marina, including some very expensive boats, and one that was set up to sell fresh seafood. The view of the industrial building they needed to assess wasn't bad, though some of the sight lines were blocked by clumps of trees and shrubs dotted along the high tide line.

"Hey folks," announced a fellow near one of the sea worthy cruisers. "We're going out on a night cruise a little later. Just 50 quid a piece if you want to come. Lots of beer and cocktails."

"Thanks, but no," Jake said.

"Maybe that's a good idea," Morgan said quietly as they continued exploring. "We could hire a private boat and do a stakeout. See what traffic is coming in here. There's probably a good reason their warehouse is so close to the water."

"A private boat's a good idea," Jake said.

They presented themselves at the marina office, once again in their newlywed middle aged couple ruse, and managed to rent a boat for two nights.

"Remember now," said the station master. "These are ocean waters, and you're not certified to sail around at all. Think of it as a floating hotel. If you want to go out, we have a crew that will take you out for a spin, or you can hire your own with the proper insurance. Let me know."

"Oh, I really hope we don't wreck this thing," Morgan said as she checked out the galley of their 30-foot cruiser. "It's way above my paygrade and looks brand new in here."

"She's got some high-tech security," Jake said. "Cameras, alarm. I'm happy."

They arranged with the station master to take the boat out the following afternoon and evening, and asked Stan to arrange the crew. Morgan signed the necessary paperwork and Stan transferred a king's ransom for a damage deposit on the cruiser.

That night, they had supper in Liverpool and returned to the boat with some Guinness and snacks. They sat on the deck together and Jake adjusted the cameras while they chatted and munched. Morgan did her best to do some focussed listening, and she shook her head in frustration.

"It's just not working," she said. "I'm not getting anything."

"Be patient," Jake said.

Morgan did the mature thing and stuck her tongue out at him. "Usually when I have a vision I'm either fast asleep, or my adrenaline's up because I'm on a job, or scared witless. I'm too relaxed." She laughed. "Imagine. I'm relaxed."

"What do you need? A nap? Or a good scare?"

"I think I need to just focus for a few seconds, and get in the zone. Hold on."

Morgan moved to the edge of the bench, and remembered sitting in Helen Davies' parlour. The lights in that room threw a yellow glare on everything, giving Ms. Davies a kind of ghastly pallor. There was always a fire in the grate even when it was warm out, and there was a never-ending supply of tea. The room was scented with citrus. Lance, the inside Rottweiler, was sometimes leaning on Morgan's legs as if to say everything would be okay. But the dog was on edge, and so was Helen, as was Morgan. In the next moment, Morgan caught herself looking into Ms. Davies' living room from outside, as if she was viewing from behind the lens of a camera while the hair on her arms stood at attention. She was in the zone.

"Okay, I've got it," she said quietly to Jake.

Jake moved over so she could peer into the computer he had set up, and look at the cameras. She donned the headset and listened closely.

"Okay, in that conversation there, just tune the speakers a bit if you can Jake."

"I...I don't have any speakers set up Morgan."

"You don't?"

"Nope."

"Well, I can hear more chatter than I ever thought possible, but it's kind of quiet."

"Can you understand any of it?"

"No, it's too faint, but I think it's coming from the buildings down the way, the ones we are after."

"Can you tune in at will do you think? Maybe try listening to something nearer first. The party boat is a lot closer than the warehouse."

Morgan nodded at him, and picked up the binoculars. Seeing what she needed to hear seemed like a good idea.

"Jeez, there're a lot of people on that boat. They must be over capacity. I think there are at least 30 people on deck," she said.

Jake was watching with her through his own binoculars.

Morgan began a commentary. "There's a guy making the move on a woman at the bow. He's being disgusting. There's a woman at the bar asking for a Mai Tai. Do people still drink those? Someone asking for a snort...I assume that's going to be cocaine. The staff are having a huddle about the boat being too full. Ha, I knew that already."

Jake put his arm gently on Morgan's forearm. "You can hear all that from here? Are you pulling my leg?"

"I can hear all of it," Morgan said, looking at him. "This superpower is going to be freaking awesome! Thank you Helen Davies and Grandad Jimmy!" She laughed, and opened another beer.

CHAPTER 34

Their two man crew were experienced and looked like a serious pair of men as they made their way to the boat. Lewis was a former colleague of Jake's – a retired MI-5 agent with 30 years of experience etched on his face. Their co-pilot, Franklin, was an active MI-5 agent with some nasty looking scars on his forearm, the result of being trapped in a burning car a few years ago. They were both in excellent physical shape, and their faces were tanned, lightly lined, and clean shaven. Lewis was the stockier of the two, and stood tall and straight like a military man. His close cropped salt and pepper hair and trim moustache gave him the look of a sergeant major, Morgan thought.

Franklin was taller, slender, and had his head tilted to one side all the time. Morgan wondered if he had to keep himself bent to fit in different places. He was a little taller than Jake when he stood straight, and Morgan gently reminded them both to pay attention when they went below deck so they didn't knock themselves out on the low doorways.

Lewis and Franklin stowed their gear as Jake finished setting up cameras with night vision and zoom capability that would make anyone within their sites look close enough to touch. He had Morgan check the screens, and she nodded her satisfaction with it all.

As they let the mooring ropes go, Morgan looked at Jake with her eyebrows furrowed. "I don't hear anything over there at all," she said, nodding toward the warehouses.

"Do you need some space to focus and get tuned in?"

"Maybe. I'll go below for a few minutes. Call if you need me."

Morgan slid her hands down the ladder for a quick descent to the galley, grabbed herself a Diet Pepsi from the fridge, and then headed toward the center of the deck to her stateroom. It was a small space, but very efficient. She heard the engine accelerate as the boat moved from its mooring and navigated through the marina. Once they got past the jetty, they'd do some cruising and tour the coastline for a couple of hours. In between looking like they were having a nice tour, there would be some heavy listening going on.

Morgan closed the door and perched on the edge of the bunk. Her feet were just off the floor and she crossed her ankles for a moment, but the boot knife tucked into her hikers wasn't very comfortable that way, so she uncrossed them and pulled the blade out of its sleeve.

The knife was new, and Morgan liked the weight of it. It was a small dagger she had found at a market in Ireland while she was healing and wandering the countryside with Jake. The blade was short enough to be allowed through her checked luggage if needed. The hilt was silver, with Celtic styled knots to help stop the blade from sinking completely into something soft. She'd sharpened the blade to get the edge on it she wanted and it could slice a piece of tomato thin enough to see through, or stop a bad guy with ease. It was heavy enough she always knew where it was in her boot.

She took a few deep breaths and looked at her reflection in the blade. *Winfeld,* she thought, *it's time to put on your cape and do this thing. Lean in, just like Ms. Davies said.*

A memory was knocking at the edge of her periphery. She found herself back in the sitting room with Ms. Davies.

They were working on leaning in, and Morgan could see the sweatered man, but couldn't figure out who he was. As if in the room with her, she heard Ms. Davies' voice loudly in her head, "Be on the lookout for someone looking out for you," the voice said.

On the lookout for me, Morgan thought. *Interesting.* She closed her eyes and thought of Jake, Lewis, and Franklin on the upper deck. She pictured them in her mind, then let herself lean back on the rail and watch them work. They were talking about navigating through the marina, the boat, and how it handled. *That's good,* Morgan thought. *I've got them tuned in; now let's stretch further afield and get into that warehouse.*

The voices came to her like radio show off an old-fashioned recording. They were distorted and tinny, but they were definitely there. She headed back up to the top deck to see if she could hear them better.

"Got your ears on okay?" Jake asked.

"Yup, the signal's up. Let's get this party started," Morgan said.

She sat at a small table at the rear of the boat and put her pop can in a recessed cup. She pulled her earbuds out of her pocket so their crewmates would think she was listening via the equipment instead of freaking them out with the listening ability she had.

Morgan could hear snatches of conversation from the warehouse, but nothing noteworthy to begin with. Liverpool accents, and then someone speaking English with a Russian accent. They switched to speaking in Russian, and Morgan couldn't keep up.

"Jake, they've switched to Russian and I can't follow the conversation."

"I speak Russian," Lewis offered helpfully. "Let me have a listen."

"Um...you can't Lewis. Sorry. The equipment isn't picking this up," Morgan explained. "Please don't panic... but I can hear them in my head."

Lewis was about to say something, then he let his breath out slowly. "Alright," he said. "Not sure what I can do...unless there's maybe a word you hear clearly that's being repeated and I can translate it for you."

"So far, I've got four different voices, but I'm sure there are more people in the building. There is a lot of static, like there's equipment in there. A lot of it."

"This area is always under watch with the police. There have been big smuggling busts here in the past, but not only drugs. Human trafficking, weapons, you name it and they'll try to get it through here. I'm surprised our cruiser hasn't been spotted by a police boat yet, to be honest," Franklin offered.

"We've been invited here officially because the police here are too recognizable, so they know we are in the area although not what we're up to specifically," Jake said.

"I'm hearing a word like *o'goine*," Morgan said.

"Fire," said Jake and Lewis together.

"It's not that there is a fire," Morgan clarified. "They are talking about fire."

"Anything else?" Lewis said.

"They are talking about drugs," Morgan said. "I just heard *weed* and *fentanyl* in English, in the middle of Russian sentences."

"What about a drone?" Franklin asked from where he steered the boat. "We could float one around if you think it might help."

"Might work, if the electronic noise I'm hearing isn't blocking signals. Let's try and get a better position relative to the warehouse and see what we get. Are you guys ready to get out the fishing gear?"

The boat was well supplied with fishing tackle, including rods and gear for deep sea fishing. None of the four members of the team knew what to do with it, but they made a good show of taking it out, dropping a couple of lines over the back end of the boat, and putting their feet up as if they were on an expensive holiday.

Morgan sat in concentration near the centre of the deck and sighed with relief when the Englishman joined the conversation and the Russians switched to English. She listened for about ten minutes, and then spoke with the team.

"It looks like these guys are a hub for internet based drug orders. They have a shipment coming in, not sure when, and then there are several computers running where they are taking online orders. I can't tell if the drugs are only for distribution in the UK or not."

"We should just go in and blow the place up then," Franklin said. His eyes lit up at the thought of getting some field action after receiving a reconnaissance assignment.

"Now, now," Lewis said. "You do remember what a recce assignment and gathering intel means."

"Course I do," Franklin said, pretending to be hurt, "But the four of us working for a couple of hours could get it looked after. Besides, I could use a little action."

"Except it'll be an international incident with the Russians, and no telling what collateral damage there could be," Morgan said with her eyebrow arched. "Maybe we need to find you some different action."

"Fine, then leave me to my fishing, won't you?"

When they pulled into the marina later that night, they secured the boat with a sophisticated set of booby traps and alarms that would awaken the team but not let intruders know. The decided to post a watch, too, just in case.

Morgan headed to her bunk to shut her eyes for a bit, and to set her alarm so she could relieve Lewis, who took the first watch. As she rolled up in her blankets, her mind went back to what she'd heard going on at the warehouse. Clearly, this was a big drug warehouse operation, but she couldn't figure out who was in charge: the British or the Russians. As she drifted into an uneasy sleep, she also realized they must have very tight security set up there, because there were no dogs and no security apparent from the outside. *The security was probably all electronic*, she thought as she drifted off to sleep. Two hours later, she woke up to her alarm feeling neither rested nor refreshed.

Up on deck, and alone for the first time since they had started this operation, Morgan could feel the chill enveloping her. There wasn't much to see in the fog and dark. She shivered as she sat down and took a sip from her flask. The Scotch warmed her a little, and she poured a shot into her coffee to make sure she stayed awake and didn't freeze. She walked slowly around the deck, listening for signs of trouble around the marina, but everything was quiet.

Morgan sat down and faced the warehouse as she sipped her spiked coffee. Soon, she heard the electronic buzzing, which she decided had to be signal blocking of some kind, and then she could hear snoring. Regular snoring, and then irregular snorts and sniffles at a slightly higher pitch.

Two people on site sleeping, she thought. She let her mind wander to the building, and looked at the access points. A large bay door big enough to let a semi-trailer in, and beyond it was an open space with two armoured looking Escalade SUVs and a Jeep Sahara. Office doors, and security cameras with their red lights blinking in quick rhythm. She could see laser beams at all angles throughout the building, making sure that any movement inside would set off the alarm. The sleeping drug traffickers were in the right hand corner at the back of the building in what appeared to be a staff room with a couple of folding cots. She could see the outlines of automatic weapons stored under their beds.

Jake joined Morgan on deck, smiling a greeting as he took the chair beside her. She nodded back to him, careful not to talk and break the stillness that surrounded them. They sat for a few minutes, until he rubbed his hand across her shoulders to chase the chill off.

"You alright?" he asked.

"Yeah. I just took a tour of that place in my head, and I don't know whether to trust what I can see or not, but it's a fortress in there." She passed him her notebook where she had drawn some crude sketches.

"What're these lines?" he indicated the criss cross pattern in her diagram.

"They're laser beams."

Jake let out a slow hiss of breath. "We are not set up to take this on."

158

"We aren't supposed to take it on, remember. This is a recce mission."

"Can we tell Stan and the director what you've seen?"

"Unless I get in there, I don't know if it's all real or not. And, if we do decide to go in and start irritating these guys, they could just open up a new warehouse on the next block."

"What about the recce? Observe and report?" He cocked an eyebrow at her, teasing, but didn't miss the down to business tone in her voice.

"Oh, we're going to report all this. Then we are going to propose an action plan. If we can mess things up enough, it should stop what is in the warehouse from getting out onto the street, and it'll force them to bring in more supplies, but the local cops will be expecting it and have a better chance of intercepting, especially with their anti-drug agents and military helping them. It's a good plan."

"Alright then, let's get Stan out of bed, and talk to the director. We've got enough gear here to disable any vehicles outside the building, set up those stun grenades for some shock value, and destroy the vehicles along with as much of the stock inside the warehouse as possible, without putting any of us on the inside. Lewis and Franklin are going to be very happy to wake up to a mission."

PART TWO

SIX MONTHS LATER

MORGAN'S JOURNAL

Monday

I didn't even know how to start a journal when the psychiatrist told me I needed one. I wasn't the journaling type. I didn't like the shrink much either. She was a softie and I didn't want to be coddled. I wanted to go cry in a corner somewhere and never come out, I'll grant you that, but I didn't want babying.

I burned the first three journals I wrote in. There was a lot of whimpering in them, and lamentations of death. There was a string of angry hangovers. Then I stopped journaling and wrote for four solid weeks. I poured my soul into a book that was written in third person instead of a journal written in first person. I continued to journal, obviously, but I found it easier to write about everything as if it was a story in the past tense. Otherwise, I couldn't stick with it.

I thought it was a decent book. I even had a publisher lined up for it, but we were having a disagreement on the day this journal starts.

You see, I needed a drink. I hadn't been drinking as much lately, and the craving hit me hard. Don't get me wrong. I like alcohol, especially a nice Scotch. But I knew I had to give it up after that last string of hangovers or I'd regret it forever. On that shitty Monday, however, I needed a big one.

I walked past the sideboard, where a bottle or two of decent but cheap Scotch normally winked at me. There was nothing. I dragged my fingers in the light layer of dust that ran across the surface, and considered whether a trip out to the liquor store was in order.

It wasn't like I had anything else to do.

I made sure the outside door to my building latched before turning down the street to the pub. I love that it's called a pub in this neighbourhood, because it's more friendly sounding, more like part of the neighbourhood than a chain of bars with a constant turnover of wait staff and bartenders. The blast of music as I opened the door hit me in the face as I left the cold, bitter street where it was Fall, and entered the welcoming heat of the bar.

"What do you have for Scotch?" I said, pulling up a seat at the bar. The bartender, very committed to customer service and quality drink, jerked his thumb over his shoulder and said, "Just the three there on the end. An ounce shot is $6, $8, or $10 depending on which one you want."

"I'll take the $8 one, make it a double. And some barbecue wings." Suddenly I was famished, but that wasn't surprising since I hadn't eaten since a bowl of cold cereal six hours beforehand.

I watched while the bartender swabbed the counter with a dubious looking rag. How could I have done so badly? I'd been over the manuscript with two different editors, and I thought it was solid work. The editors liked where it was at. It was a good story, they had both said, and now they had smoothed out the rough spots and fixed tenses and grammar, it was even better.

I touched the Scotch to my lips, and let a small sip of the nectar sit on my tongue. I liked the way it tingled, and I always tried to savour that first sip.

I looked around the bar briefly. There were a few touristy couples, a foursome that obviously worked together and liked their beer on tap, and there was an old guy sitting in the corner who made eye contact. He had a long scraggly beard, nothing like the thirty-year old's around him with their finely groomed facial hair. I dipped my head in a quick, pub style nod to say hello. He didn't nod back, and I looked away.

I had thought my book was ready, but my publisher said differently. More polish, she said.

"More polish," I had said back to her over the phone. "What does that mean? I've given my all to this book, and kept as true as I can to real life. Except for some pieces I had to cut out because they made the story unbelievable. You asked me to do that. What do you mean by more polish exactly? If you can't tell me, I don't know what I need to do."

"It's a little short for what we want to sell as a trade paperback. Add another couple of chapters, and then let's see how the editorial board likes it."

"You know that this story isn't some kind of happy ever after book. There is no nice way to wrap it up and tie a bow on it."

"I know, because in real life your man died. But he doesn't have to die in the story, does he? Maybe there's a big rescue and he survives and your heroine lives happily ever after with her man. Happens all the time."

"Happens all the time in fairy tales you mean. But this book is true, with stuff left out because it makes it more real for a reader. If I put everything into it, they'd never believe any of it."

"Well, the word from the board is that it needs to have a more memorable and significant ending, including a big kiss if you can arrange it. I need it submitted in two weeks."

As I sat at the bar recalling the conversation, I lost my appetite for the wings that were coming. I thought about Jake. We had completed a few missions together, had some great adventures, and probably would have stayed together forever if he hadn't up and died on that damned boat.

Tuesday

I called early and left my publisher a message. I was pretty sure she didn't want to end our deal, but I wanted to hear her say it.

The phone rang again, jarring me back to the present. "Hey Cuz," I said, knowing who it was from the call display.

"I'm surprised you answered," she said giggling. "I always think you block my calls."

Little did she know about my rule. My cousin Colette called nearly every week and I made a point of picking up every third or fourth call so we stayed connected, but that was the extent of my commitment.

"Not today, Colette. What're you up to?"

"Working, you know how it is, just go go go all the time! Anyway, Brian's family is coming for Thanksgiving and we thought you could join us. It's a quick trip from where you are into Maine, and we haven't seen you in forever."

"Um...I'm not really travelling at the moment. I've got things on the go here. Maybe in the new year?"

"You need to get out of your apartment. You've been stuck there for months. The extended family won't be staying with us, except for you. The rest will be in hotels, but we'll have everyone here for dinner. You can stay in the spare room, we'll drink some Scotch, and send you home with leftovers if you're lucky."

"Colette, I just...I have a lot going on...," and I didn't have the heart to tell her I didn't feel much like being all thankful just because it was Thanksgiving in America. I hadn't celebrated Canadian Thanksgiving either.

She sighed. "Don't lie to me Morgan. You don't have diddly squat going on except that you are procrastinating about your book, and I know it. How come I haven't been able to read it yet?"

"At this point I can't say when I'll be able to let some early copies out. The publisher says it needs some more spit and polish." I looked at the box with the manuscript in it, where it sat on the floor near my desk. I tapped it with my foot and kicked it under the desk. "But, I'll let you know."

"I'll call you tomorrow and see if you've changed your mind. And to tempt you with the menu. You should bring the book with you so I can read it."

Great. I could hardly wait.

It's not that I didn't like Colette, or her husband Brian. They were – and are – good people. It's just that the thought of driving seven hours to Bangor, Maine to see them and having to act all festive and social wasn't all that tempting. I looked outside and saw dark clouds gathering. How fitting. There was a storm coming alright.

Wednesday

By the time hurricane Martin hit us today, it had calmed to a tropical storm. I watched through my apartment window as the storm raged, grateful for the sound construction of the building I live in. I was so attached to this suite that I had purchased it from the agency after Jake died. The view was stunning when the sun was out, and it wasn't bad in crappy weather either. There were boats of every size and type to watch, plus restaurants, and people came and went in a steady stream. Plenty of people, 24/7. The place is called Bishop's Landing, and it offers community when I want it, and allows me to be anonymous when I don't.

During the storm, the view off my balcony on the sixth floor was like a scene from a Stephen King novel. Fog, driving rain, hail. More rain and buffeting, bitter wind. Martin had started as a category three hurricane in the Gulf Coast before it punched, wailed, and gloated its way up the eastern seaboard toward us. I wasn't worried, despite living close to the water, because I am one of those annoyingly organized people. My suite was on the sixth and top floor of the building. I wasn't going to get flooded at that height, although the elevator shafts and parking certainly could. And, I was always ready for a storm, something I attributed to my training as well as the conviction that it was stupid to be unprepared. I keep several days worth of water stored in the closet of the spare bedroom, along with ration packs of food, protein bars, and canned food that could get two people through a week of closed stores or storm cleanup. The day before Martin arrived, I had a bag of storm chips in there, too, but I caved in and ate them while sipping a Scotch and I waiting for the storm to arrive.

Storm chips are a Nova Scotia thing. Rumour (and the internet) says that a radio host named Stephanie Domet had been talking about picking up some chips and dip before a storm, and then people started talking about how buying chips was their favourite, and often the only, prep they did before a big storm. The conversation inspired people to share their chip stories, and in no time at all a local chip company started selling a bag of their (practically famous) kettle chips with four flavours mixed into one bag. I found them awful initially, but after weathering my first few Maritime weather events, storm chips became a staple in my cupboard. Along with the other stuff I needed, of course.

When Tropical Storm Martin took a break, and with Jake on my mind, I grabbed my bright blue raincoat and a ballcap to head out for a look around. I could feel beads of sweat on my lip as soon as I left the building. A storm like this brought plenty of warm air from the south with it, and it only took a minute of walking outside before I felt like I was in the tropics.

The rain had slowed to a fine drizzle, but it was blowing sideways across my vision and into my ear. I adjusted my collar to keep most of it out, and pulled my hat down as far as I could.

The buildings along the harbour were shuttered and closed. The place was deserted. Here and there was a limb off a small wiry tree, and there were hundreds of leaves stuck to the sides of the buildings. There were not many boats in the water, but the ones that were there bobbed maniacally on churning water as I looked.

After I walked around the entire outside of my building, I figured I'd walk down the harbour and see how the museum boats had fared. These were old vessels that had been converted into permanent museums for curious tourists. They too were tightly shut against the weather, and there was no obvious damage.

The wind started picking up again, so I decided to get off the waterfront, and walk toward home along Lower Water Street where there would be some protection from the wind. The pavement was buried under a thick, slippery coat of leaves. The flowers in the heavy cement planters were smashed beyond recognition, and reminded me of piles of chopped kale, though the planters were all intact.

I stopped at a curb to scrape off the layer of leaves that had stuck to the bottom of my rainboots. It took several tries to get them all off. While I fussed with the boots, I heard a snuffling noise. I thought it was probably a trick of the wind, until there was whimpering among the snuffling. Whatever it was made the sound of a small child in trouble, and I quickly wove my way around the planters to see what was going on.

The noise was coming from a young, very wet dog. I looked at the soaking mess of hair, and he looked back, his eyes pleading and frightened. It was impossible to tell what kind of dog he was, though he looked the colour of dark rum. He was tugging to get away from the planters, but stuck there by a piece of rope that was caught under one edge. As I fought to free the rope, he jumped at me, butt wiggling madly, and he left big footprints of muck on my jeans and coat.

"How long have you been out here, buddy?" I asked, pulling at the rope. It was jammed firmly under a corner of the cement planter and hard to tell if the dog had been struggling and trapped it there, or if someone had stuck him there on purpose.

"Just a minute, fella," I said, pushing him off me with one arm while trying to free the rope.

"Sit," I suggested, "let me get this out." He tried to sit for a nanosecond, but popped right up again. His rope was short, and thick as a rope used to moor a small boat might be. It was also slippery. I pulled out my knife, glad I had thought to slip it into the pocket of my raincoat. I had to hold the pup at bay with one hand and cut the rope with the other. It certainly wasn't a sanctioned type of maneuver, but it got the job done. Once the pup realized he was free he wiggled even harder. I expected him to run off wherever he had come from, but instead he pawed at my wet boot.

I know people who say they are dog or cat or horse people, and I've never been any of those things. I never wanted an animal to worry about. Ever. Not when my parents wanted one when I was a kid. And not the one suggested by a well meaning shrink, when, before entering the spy business, my husband had his plane shot down and was killed.

"Go on," I said, pointing helpfully into the distance. "Go home."

The dog continued to wiggle. "Git!" I said, again pointing to nowhere in particular. He sat that time, and looked directly at me, his brown eyes squinting in the blowing drizzle.

"Okay, let's see if you have a tag." I felt around his collar, which was old and well worn, but there was no dog tag to help identify him. The rain was getting heavier, and we were both soaked. I sighed. Having a dog in my apartment was not my idea of a good time, but I couldn't just leave him outside.

I took the end of his rope and he happily trotted alongside me, headfirst into the wind.

When we got home I called the animal shelter, but it was closed. I called a couple of vet clinics, and they had their answering machines on but were closed because of the storm. Not knowing anyone else that could help, I had to call Dave at home.

His voice was rushed on the phone. "I can't talk long Morgan. We're up to our ankles in water in the goat barn. What's happening?"

"Oh right, I forgot about the goats. Do you need help? I can come to you."

"We're good for now, and besides, the bridge you need to cross to get here is swamped. What's happening there?"

"I, um, I was out walking after the storm..."

"You mean in the storm, because you know damn well it's not finished yet, don't you?" Dave was a veterinarian, and he wasn't big on making people feel good about themselves.

"Yeah, Dave, I know. But I was out checking the neighbourhood, and I found a dog. He's youngish, big, and I need to know who he belongs to."

"Well good luck with figuring that out right now. Does he have a tag? A tattoo?"

"Dogs have tattoos?"

"Yeah, the important ones do. It might be hard to see, but it could be inside his ear, or on his belly near his back leg. Have a look and call me back if you find something and I'll look it up when I can, but not until these goats are safe."

I looked at the puppy, who was shivering despite the heat.

"Okay, buddy. Don't give up now. Let me see you." I looked in his ears, which were filthy, but I couldn't see a tattoo. He seemed to like the attention, but he was still trembling and when a blast of wind shook the building, he yelped and crawled into my lap. I could feel his ribs under his filthy coat. I patted him and let him snuggle in a bit, since my clothes were soaked and his dirty feet were all over them. I turned him over like a baby and looked around his bits for a tattoo. There was nothing, though the fact that he was a boy was obvious.

His trembling was getting worse, so I ran a bath.

"Look, dog, I have nothing puppy approved to feed you. But I do have some nice bath stuff we can treat you to."

He warmed with the bath and the trembling stopped by the time we sat on the couch afterward. I didn't have any dog brushes, so I dug out an old hairbrush and used that on him. He had a lot of hair and it started to curl as he dried.

It was still hot and humid in the apartment but he was damp despite being towelled off and brushed until my arm ached. I turned the gas fireplace on low and cracked open a window so I wasn't likely to melt. "That's just to help you dry," I told him. "I don't normally turn the fireplace on in this kind of heat." His tail thwapped against the couch cushion.

Thursday

"He's been through some kind of ordeal," Dave said. "There are some sores on his skin. His front paws are sore, he's skinny, and he's got a wicked case of earmites."

"Earmites? Is that why his ears looked dirty?"

"Yup."

"Oh gross. He's been on my couch. Those are all treatable, right? Do I need to decontaminate my apartment?"

"Yes, they are treatable, and no you don't have to worry about your apartment. Unless you had him sleeping in bed, maybe. Oh yeah, and I've got Sara checking to see if there is a report of him missing. He's a nice pup, or he will be in a few days. Someone must be looking for him."

Dave was a dear friend, and an even better vet. He'd been in the business a long time, and was well connected in the neighbourhood. Sara was his wife and office manager. They were both in their seventies and worked at the clinic full-time in between managing a small acreage that included their rescued goats.

"When are you coming over for supper?" Sara asked when she presented me the bill. "We haven't seen you in ages, Morgan."

"I know and I'm sorry. I've been..."

"Liar," Sara laughed, her silver streaked curls bouncing wildly. "I know you're not busy now you're semi-retired or whatever you are. You're too young to be doing nothing, so come and see us. We'll be rebuilding the goat enclosure at the weekend."

"Okay, what shall I bring?"

"You? Nothing honey. Except the dog I suspect."

"Oh, I'm not keeping him. You need to track down his owners. He can't stay at my condo. Dogs aren't even allowed in the building." *And they can pay the vet bill*, I thought, as I handed her my credit card to cover the $300 bill.

"Don't get your hopes up on the dog going anywhere. There's nothing listed in the missing pets, and he's not even microchipped," she smiled as she zipped my card through the reader.

"Sara," I whispered across the counter to her. "I'm not a dog person, and you know that."

"Coulda fooled me." She laughed, passing me a dog lead with the puppy attached to it. He licked my hand.

"Knock that off," I said. "There will be no licking."

I went home with a bag of puppy appropriate food, and a couple of cans of canned food to help transition him off the people food I'd fed him for two days. Of course, when I put the vet approved dog food down in front of him, he sniffed it and then looked at me sadly. The night before he'd scoffed down half a package of beef jerky, and for breakfast I'd microwaved him some scrambled eggs.

"Sorry pal. Doctor's orders. You have to eat it or starve, and you're kinda skinny, so get on with it."

He laid on the floor, his paws just touching the edge of the bowl, and stared up at me. There was no missing the disappointment in his face.

After he laid there staring at the dish for awhile, I started to worry. Dave had mentioned more than once how skinny the pup was. I took a piece of cheese from the fridge and he sniffed approvingly until I squished it into his food. He returned to staring.

I sat on the floor beside him and patted his head. "You need a name buddy. I can't keep calling you 'dog.' I'm sure you have a name. You're cute. You're pretty loveable. I really wish your people would show up. That'd make this a lot easier. I found you in a storm, so that could work...but maybe it's too corny. How about Howard?"

I swear he rolled his eyes with that one. "George?"

Nothing.

"How about Maverick? You seem to be a free spirit. And you're not tattooed or branded. You're pretty much the definition of a maverick, so let's try that and see how it works?" He put his head on my hand, and wagged his tail gently.

Saturday

Maverick has started to adjust to being in the apartment. He is potty trained, thankfully, but he has a horrible habit of waking at 4:30 and whining as if he has to pee urgently. It took me a couple of these early mornings to realize he could hear things starting to stir outside and just wanted to go see what was going on. I am feeling deprived of some beauty sleep, so I called the animal shelters again, the local TV station, and every veterinarian I could find. No one has reported the dog as missing.

This morning, he woke at 4:30 and stood beside my bed, butt wiggling. I reached over to him, and pointed to the blanket in the corner that counted as his bed. No reaction except more butt wiggling and then some whining. I leaned over and picked him up awkwardly. He seemed to be all legs and licking tongue, and I settled him down at the end of my bed, hoping he'd catch on and settle back down to sleep. He didn't stay there long, but once he was up at the top of the bed with his head on the pillow beside mine, he fell asleep and slept until six.

"Dave," I said into the phone. "I need to know if you have a place for Maverick. He's getting settled in here, and I don't want him to."

"You named him," Dave laughed. "He's yours. And before you get mad, there are no reports of anyone missing an eight month old golden retriever pup, so you should probably register him with the city so you don't get a ticket."

"Register him? No way! I'm not even allowed to have him in my condo. And I don't want a dog."

"You know that little acreage down the road from here is still for sale. Might be perfect for you and Maverick."

"I already have a place Dave. A place I like, thank you very much. Where I don't have to ride a tractor to cut the grass, or pick up dog poop, or wash the outside windows, or tend a garden."

"Yeah, well you might have to rethink that uppity place you bought on the harbour so the dog doesn't feel rejected. See you later. We are starting on the goat barn in an hour," he said as he rang off.

I searched Facebook for lost dog messages. Again, there was nothing. As I closed the lid on my laptop, I heard a noise at my feet. Maverick was trying to dig the manuscript out from under the desk where it has sat since I kicked it there.

I got up and kicked it back where it belonged.

"Don't eat that. And while we're at it, don't eat anything that doesn't have your name on it," I said.

He wagged his tail and dug some more. I decided it was time for a walk, and picked up a chewed shoe from the mat at the door. "Oh, now you've done it," I said, "you chewed my favourite running shoe!" I shook it in Maverick's general direction, and dug around in the closet for another pair. I shook those at him too, and said, "No chewing!" in my boss voice. He had the good sense to look sheepish.

Ninety minutes later, I arrived at Dave and Sara's just as several other helpers pulled up to the acreage on the outskirts of Halifax county. The place was a beautiful mess, the big estate home standing strong among downed trees and puddles of standing water. The air smelled of wet earth and ocean.

"About time you got here," Dave said. "The dog kennel is open for the dog. You probably won't want him in the goat barn."

Maverick's nose was in overdrive as he caught scent of the goat barn, and then he saw the goats. There were 12 of them in a temporary enclosure, where one was standing on an abandoned car, and others were staring from the top of a picnic table. They were making a racket that had Maverick tilting his head from side to side as he tried to make out their odd sounds and smells.

"This is grunt work today," Dave said, "But I know how much you love being in charge, so if you can wrangle a few of those guys there, we need to set up the pumps here and then see what's left of the place. I'm not sure if we can save the walls or not, but we'll have a better idea once they aren't sitting in pools of water."

The barn looked as though a water cannon had been set to it. The water was well over my ankles, and the building was cold with all the power shut off and no lights or heat available. "You and you," I said, pointing to a pair of capable looking young men that were gaggling outside the barn. "Let's get to work."

"Yes ma'am!" One of them smiled and said quickly. "I'm Paul, and this is my brother Jean. We just need to know what you want us to do."

"Well," I said, taking in the fact that these two hadn't balked at the idea of taking orders and looked happy to help, "We need to get all this water in here pumped out to the drainage pond and then there will be piles of dirt and silt to move."

"Okay," Jean said. "Let's go."

The hoses were awkward, and the generators heavy. Paul and Jean worked hard, and talked the entire time, mostly to each other. They were Dave's nephews, twins, and normally worked together at their construction company, Two Heads Four Arms, based in the Annapolis Valley.

"Can't thank you enough for helping us today," I said cheerfully. Getting used to telling people what to do outside of the agency was a challenge for me, and I was making a point of trying to chat.

"We're happy to help," Paul said. "Dave's our uncle and if it hadn't been for him and Sara, we'd probably both be on pogey or in jail."

"That sounds like Dave and Sara, from what I know of them." I handed him a coil of hose.

"If you hear stories, they are all true," Jean chimed in. "When we were kids and our mom died from cancer, we gave our dad a real hard time for a few years."

"You sure as hell did," Dave said, poking his head into the barn door. "You all set up in here? Need anything?"

"No, we're good, Dave," I said. "We should have the water drained pretty quick. The silt could be another matter though."

"Alright," Dave said. "I'm going to set up some scaffolding outside and we'll get on the roof to see what things are looking like up top."

By the end of the day the water was pumped out of the barn and in the holding pond or headed downhill. There was plenty of damage to the walls, which had wicked up water, silt, and were already sporting mold. We were discussing the logistics of tearing the barn down when,

175

from out of nowhere it seemed, one of the neighbours showed up with several large containers of chilli and some fresh buns.

We gathered around the porch, eating out of plastic bowls.

"That was a good day's work," Sara said to the team. "Thank you all so much. We really couldn't do it without you."

There were nods and waves from the assembled group.

"Happy to help," Jean said. "Eh! Whose dog is there terrorizing the squirrel?"

I looked over to see Maverick stretched as tall as he could get reaching up a tree with his back feet on the ground. He was not bothered at all that the squirrel was swearing and chirping loudly at him.

"Hey Morgan," Dave said. "Isn't that your dog?"

"He's not mine," I protested, handing my bowl to Dave. "Hold this for a sec," I said stepping onto the lawn. "Maverick, Maverick, come here."

The dog dragged itself away from the excitement, and stood in front of me. "No chewing the squirrels," I said, and I pulled his dirty tennis ball from my pocket and tossed it in the other direction. He merrily chased it, the squirrel off his mind for the time being.

When I returned to the porch, Dave handed my chilli back to me.

"He's doing really well, you know," Dave said, "You just called a puppy off a squirrel and he engaged in ball toss. That's not easy."

"I told you he is smart and loveable," I said. "He needs a home where someone can include him in a family. And he still needs some manners. He's already eaten one of my good runners, a blanket, and he chewed the cuff off of my favourite sweater."

Jean had overheard the conversation. "Are you really looking for a place for him? You aren't going to keep him?"

"No, I can't keep him where I am and I'm surprised no one at the condo has complained yet, honestly. Dogs aren't allowed, and I'm not a dog person anyway. He needs a home."

Jean looked at me, his mid-twenties face still unlined, his dark thick brows furrowed over deep brown eyes and a crooked nose. "Maybe he needs you as much as you need him."

"I don't need a dog. What I need is for someone to want this dog," I said.

"Well, if you're sure. Dad needs a dog, don't you think so Paul?"

"He needs a dog like I need a hole in my head. What makes you think Dad needs a dog?" Paul looked similar to his brother, although he had missed the puck that broke his brother's nose in a winter game of pond hockey the previous year.

"Dad's alone, has been for years. He can't meet a woman if he never gets out of the house," Jean said.

"So, you think if Dad gets a dog, he'll meet a woman?" Paul said, frowning.

"Something like that. You know, he's a nice guy and it sucks that he's been a widower for fifteen years, and he's never been on a date. I think a dog is a good way to get him out so he can meet some people."

"Maverick needs a lot of walking, and he is very friendly," I said, hoping that would help. "Maybe he could help your dad if you think he's up for meeting new people."

"He used to be," Dave said. "He and Marie, his wife, were always out in the community and knew everyone. That's a good idea, Jean. Maybe he could take the dog for a trial and see how they do."

"No trial," I said. "Maverick needs a home, and I need to reclaim mine."

"Who is going on trial?" a tall, slender, greying man asked. He grabbed a beer from the cooler as he approached.

"No one," Paul said. "We were just talking with Morgan about her dog. Well, it's a dog Morgan rescued during the storm. No owners have claimed him, and me and Jean think he'd be perfect for you."

"You think I need a dog?" he said, smiling patiently at his sons.

"Yes," Dave offered. "So, you can get out of your house more often and meet some people. It's possible that if you are out walking a dog you may even meet yourself a girlfriend. Speaking of meeting people, Morgan, meet Daniel. He's the dad that Paul and Jean share."

"Nice to meet you Daniel. Would you like to meet Maverick?"

"Well, I was thinking about getting a dog, or starting up some kind of hobby, but not to meet women. More for company." He laughed a hearty laugh, and his boys joined in.

Daniel, Paul, and Jean were sleeping at Dave's that night since they lived so far away. I was returning to my apartment and we had all agreed that in the morning I would bring Maverick back with the gear he'd accumulated, so he could go to his new home.

Sunday

Last night, my dreams were back and I tossed and turned in bed, trying not to wake the dog. I hadn't remembered a dream in months, and frankly I was happy that dreams of people being burned, or shot, or...whatever...had taken a hiatus.

"Maybe it's just because I ate all that chilli, Maverick." I rubbed his head and hoped he'd go back to sleep. He sighed, and put his head back down on the pillow.

After another half hour of tossing, I got up and grabbed my travel mug from the coffee maker. We weren't allowed to run together yet, and so I carried coffee with me so I could sip while Maverick trotted around. Dave had warned me that as a puppy, and especially a big breed, my typical runs were too long for Maverick. Instead, I let the dog set the pace for our walk and off we went.

When we got home, I calculated the time in Wales and called my friend, and cousin, Helen Davies.

"How are you, my darling?" Her voice was soft. "I've been wondering about you this week. How are you fairing? Are ye okay?"

I was making a coffee as I called her, and poured a small shot of Scotch into it. "I'm…I'm doing okay Helen, thanks for asking…well, to be honest it's really been lonely."

"Why don't you come here for a holiday? Take a break. Soak in some fresh air and eat until you can't squeeze anymore in?"

"I have lots of fresh air here, Helen," I said. "I can't get away just now. We've just had a big storm here and I'm helping friends fix up their place. Plus, I have a dog I'm temporarily looking after."

"You? You got yourself a dog?" I could hear her stifling a laugh.

"Well…I found him during the storm and I haven't been able to track down his owners, but I did find someone who is going to take him later today."

"Oh girl, Gareth will be so jealous! So tell me then, why are you calling out of the blue? Bad dream?"

I updated her quickly. "You remember when we first met and you were teaching me about how to control my dreams? Lean in and look closely?"

"Aye, of course I do."

"Well, I haven't had dreams for months. Not since Jake died, and I had one last night that was a doozy. It was like a rock concert in intensity, but a lot of different scenes from the past, only with massive amounts of colour and noise. It was a very loud dream, and I never had that before."

"Just pick one element at a time to focus on. If the colour is prevalent, focus on that. Turn it down or freeze it, then focus on the noise. And stop eating spicy food before bed and that'll probably help."

"Thanks Helen. You always know exactly what to say." As I hung up I realized that I hadn't mentioned a thing about eating chilli last night.

I shook off the past as thoughts of Jake knocked at the back of my mind, and patted Maverick's head.

I looked down, where Maverick had been licking the carpet. "Stop licking the rug Maverick. That's gross." That silly dog would lick just about anything if he could. The floor, the side of the couch while he laid on the floor, and even the leg of my pants. I scooped up his toys, poop bags, and decided to throw in the blanket he'd been using as a bed. He watched me with his head cocked to one side as if he understood this was moving day for him.

I reached Dave and Sara's by 8:30 as everyone was finishing breakfast. The kitchen smelled of bacon, and Maverick and I both looked for some leftovers.

"You aren't feeding him bacon, Morgan?" Dave asked in a tone that said he had seen me sneak the dog a piece.

"Only a little, Dave." I smiled sweetly. "Is that bad?"

"Yes, it's too high in fat. Here, give him this instead." He handed me a big cookie that looked homemade.

"Sara make these?" I asked. I gave it a sniff and wanted to test a bit because it smelled of oats and peanut butter, just like a breakfast cookie should.

"Yup, she makes all that stuff around here. She accomplishes so much she makes me feel like I am standing still," he said.

"Who's standing still?" Sara said as she walked into the kitchen. "Anyone standing around will get a job to do!" She laughed her big open laugh, her short grey curls emphasizing the happiness in this place. Suddenly I needed to get outside.

"Good morning Sara," I said. "I'll just take him out on the deck with this so he isn't making a mess in your kitchen." As I maneuvered the dog out the door, I heard Sara say, "We need to find her someone. If she doesn't have that dog, and nobody to go home to, she's going to..." and then I shut the door so I couldn't hear the rest. I knew what they were saying anyway. It's not like I hadn't thought about it myself.

I'd lost my husband so long ago that sometimes I wasn't sure the memories of him were mine. After a while, I needed to fill the void so I'd joined the agency and trained in covert operations. After time honing my skills and becoming a pretty decent spy, I met Jake. We worked well together because we shared everything, including the most intimate parts of our lives.

Then one day, after we had done highly effective stakeouts and listening from a boat off the coast of England, and just as we were preparing to mount an assault on a heavily fortified drug warehouse, Jake had a massive heart attack and fricking died. Just like that. If he hadn't have dropped right before my eyes, I would have thought his death was a story made up by the agency. But, even with paramedics and paddles and extensive CPR, he didn't wake up.

Maverick was tugging at the bottom of my pantleg, breaking me out of my reverie. He was finished his cookie and ready for something new to do.

"Alright buddy," I said, "Let's go see if your new family is here."

I delivered Maverick along with all his gear to his newly adopted dad, and then headed to the goat barn with Paul and Jean so we could start tearing down the walls.

"You will miss that sweet puppy, no?" Jean said.

"Probably," I tried to smile at Jean, but I knew it came out as a grimace since I was trying not to cry. And why would I cry anyway, I asked myself. It was just a dog.

"It's okay boss," Paul said, throwing his arm casually around my shoulders. "Our father is an equal opportunity kind of guy. You can visit Maverick whenever you want."

"Thanks guys," I said. "Now let's get on with this and make some noise."

I stayed and worked as long as I could at the goat barn, and the sun was well down as I pulled away from Sara and Dave's acreage and headed home. I had enough chilli leftovers in a cooler bag on the front seat of my car to feed me for three days. Sara always thought I was going to starve to death and liked to load me up with food when I was there.

"It's not that I don't eat – I just don't cook much anymore," I had protested, but Sara wouldn't hear of it.

"Now you've got that dog sorted, I know you'll be out running like a mad woman every chance you get," she said, "and you'll need to eat. You know me, I always worry that you are starving."

"I don't starve, Sara. You know how I like to eat. It's just that cooking holds no appeal for me at all."

I stopped myself from pulling back as Sara put her warm, dry hand on my face. "So much loss for you," she said. "I don't know how you do it."

"How she does what," Paul asked as he came into the kitchen and grabbed a crusty bun from the basket by the sink.

"I was just saying that I don't know how Morgan does it. She gets up every day and puts her nose to the grindstone and I don't know that I could do the same after all that loss."

"Well," Paul said, with all the confidence of a fellow in his mid-twenties who had experienced some loss himself, "It sure beats the alternative, doesn't it?"

"What alternative is that?" Sara asked, cocking her eyebrow at him and one hand on her hip.

"Death," he confirmed.

"You got that right," I said. "Most of the time, anyway."

I kissed Sara on the cheek, nodded to Paul, and set off to return to a quiet and empty apartment.

Monday

I pulled out the vacuum and got to work first thing. Even though the dog was only here a short time, there were clumps of light fluffy hair throughout the place. I swooped around doing my best imitation of someone who has solid domestic skills, until I hit the box under my desk. I bent down to fish it out and sat on my haunches contemplating what to do with it.

My publisher had said it needed some spit and polish. I still didn't know what she meant, and then I had an idea. She had, of course, taken a red pen and made a few notes here and there. Mostly, the page margins were empty and there was a single check mark at the end of each page.

I booted up my computer, and opened the file creatively called "Book: Version 12" and then compared it with two notes she had written on the manuscript. One called for insertion of a comma, so I did that. The other note highlighted an awkward sentence, so I changed it into two short sentences. I didn't make any other changes. She hadn't given me any other clues to what I should do to spit and polish it, so I printed Version 13, placed it back into the box, and prepared it for the post office.

Next, I needed to book a trip to Wales. I checked my calendar which was, of course, empty. The phone rang, and startled me. *Gawd*, I thought as I answered the phone, *I need a drink.*

I recognized the number on my screen, and wondered why Director Steeves was calling.

"Winfeld," I said by way of answer, so he'd know he'd called me, hopefully by mistake.

"Morgan," a voice I didn't recognize said. "This is Director Mullins, we haven't met yet but I need to speak with you about something important."

"Where's Director Steeves?" I asked. Steeves had been good to work with, and a good ambassador for the agency and the work we did.

"Director Steeves has been promoted, and he is now Chief Administrator here. He's in the situation room and can't make this call. He asked me to call you. We'd like to invite you back to work if you are ready."

"Ready, um, Mullins...You know that I retired, right?"

"Well yes, that's the story I heard, but I also heard..." he cleared his throat nervously, "I heard that you retired when your partner died. We are hoping that you are now ready to come back. We could use your help."

"I'm...," *not interested*, I thought. "I'm not considering doing anything right now, Director Mullins. Except maybe a little travelling. Maybe catching up on some reading. That kind of thing."

"I see. I should tell Steeves that you aren't interested, then?"

"Correct."

"Alright. I wish you'd really consider what I have to say."

"Find someone else Director. I'm retired."

I felt a fleeting pang of guilt as I hung up the phone. I had absolutely nothing else to do now, aside from obsessively cleaning my empty apartment.

I went to the kitchen contemplating making another pot of coffee. I knew the caffeine wasn't really something I needed, but I had a chill and wanted to chase if off without alcohol. I put the coffee on and went to the door to answer a knock. It was the property manager.

"Come on in," I said. "I just put a pot of coffee on."

"Thanks," she said, sitting herself on the edge of the couch. She clearly had something on her mind.

"The coffee is going to be a minute, but you obviously have something to say. Want to get it off your chest?" I thought I was about to catch hell about the dog, and I was ready for it.

She cleared her throat. She was a small, round woman. Five feet if I was being kind. She wore her hair short, in a straight bob that had been expertly cut. She used her beautifully manicured hand to tuck her hair behind her ear.

"Paula, you're nervous. Don't be. What's up?" I sat across from her on the couch where Jake had sat and stroked my arm after I had been shot. The memory felt surreal, as if it was part of someone else's life.

"Well," she started, "this is harder than I thought."

"Just spit it out," I laughed. "The tension is killing me...if it's about the dog, I found him a home and he's gone already."

"You...you had a dog in here?" Paula asked, her eyebrows lifted. She covered her mouth to stop a laugh spilling out. Her red nails were an exact colour match to her lipstick.

"Yeah, I thought you were coming to give me crap for that. I found him during the storm and just found him a new home."

She laughed, a high nervous laugh. "Oh hell no, I don't care if you had a dog, although I didn't even notice." She paused, and looked at me with her dark blue eyes. "We want your condo."

"You want my condo? What, you mean you want to lease it out? Buy it?"

"Yes, I mean, we'd like to make you an offer and buy it. Don't get me wrong. We love having you here. And you could sell this suite and then buy one on the floor below so you'd be near the top but not on the top floor."

"Huh?" I said, standing up to fetch the coffee. "Keep talking while I pour."

"Well, our company would like to turn the entire top floor into a penthouse. The elevator would come up right into the suite, and they'd have a panoramic view, tons of space. It'd be one of the best places to live in Halifax."

"I love this place Paula. You guys all know that I put myself into financial distress buying it, but I did that because I don't want to lose it."

"Well, you could buy the new place. It'll be huge, and stunning. Wait until you see the plans!"

"I don't need to see the plans, I already love this place."

"But what you love is the view, and the location. This suite is looking dated and a total renovation would be amazing."

"What's the cost of the new place?" I asked.

"Don't you want to hear what I can offer you for this place, first?"

"No, I want to hear what you would list the penthouse for. What do you think it's worth?"

"We're thinking the asking price would be around $3.8 million."

"What...are you shitting me?"

She pretended to blush at my cussing, even though I'm pretty sure she could dish it out if needed.

"No...not at all," she said.

"Do you have a buyer already?"

"No, although you're the only person on this floor I haven't spoken to about it."

"So...you want to buy the properties on this floor, gut them, and then sell one big super suite."

"There's only you and one other suite on this floor that we need to buy. The others are ours already, and we lease them out as long term suites, like this one was before you bought it."

I let that sink in a bit. I love this place. I like being close to the harbour. I like being in the energy and on top of the water. But maybe this was an opportunity for me to move on, after all.

"Okay," I said, adding a tot of Scotch to my coffee, and extending the bottle to her. "How much are you offering?"

"$850,000 and we'll cover legal and closing costs." She shuddered as she got the taste of strong alcohol with her coffee.

"That's not enough, Paula. I have to move, remember."

"But you didn't even have to buy anything when you moved in here. It came furnished. And I know what you paid for it."

So did I. I had paid $650,000 for the apartment, but the mortgage was enormous despite me putting every dime I had into it.

"Paula, I know your boss will have given you an upper limit and you wouldn't lead with it. How much room do you have to negotiate?"

"If you get me another coffee without any of that booze in it, I'll tell you," she said.

I jumped up and headed for the pot. "We can do one of two things," she said. "We can buy your place, and then you can buy the new condo. Or we can negotiate something."

"I am not spending just shy of $4 million for a condo Paula. No way. Even if the book I wrote becomes a best-seller I couldn't afford it, and what on earth would I do with an entire floor? It'd be a huge cavern of empty space."

"How do you feel about a million dollars, and you leave the furniture?" she asked.

"I think that will work. When do you want possession?"

"Fifteen days."

I shook her hand.

As Paula left, the phone rang again. *This will be Steeves*, I thought, and I wasn't disappointed.

"Morgan," he said. "It's good to hear your voice."

"Congratulations on your promotion," I said, and I meant it.

"Morgan, I won't beat around the bush. We could use your help, and we need it fast."

"Well, I just sold my condo. Where and when?"

"I'll book you a flight so you can meet with me and Director Mullins. Do you have things you need to tidy up there, or can I book you on the first flight out?"

"First flight is fine, but first class would be nice."

He laughed, and we signed off. As I tapped my cell to disconnect, it dawned on me that this was why the dreams had returned. It was time to get back to work.

Wednesday

London was cold and wet when I arrived, just like the rest of England. I was travelling light, with just a backpack and very squishable clothing. It was enough to keep me in clean clothes for three days as long as I wasn't required to dress up. I grabbed a taxi at Gatwick airport and went straight to the office in jeans, ankle boots, my standard black t-shirt, and my well worn leather jacket.

"Winfeld!" Steeves called out, appearing from the background before I presented myself to the receptionist. He gave me a big hug, something he had never done before, and introduced me to Director Mullins as I clipped a visitor badge to my lapel.

Mullins and I shook hands.

"Come in this way. We'll talk in my office," Mullins said.

"In the years I worked for the agency, I never got to see this office. You always came out to see us in the field." I looked at Steeves for an explanation.

He nodded. "This place is much safer than meeting outside these days. It was built as a bunker and used by Winston Churchill in WW2. We have great security and intel gathering capacity here, that I want you to see."

Mullins pulled out a bottle of Scotch and three glasses as we sat down at the round table in his office. I held up my hand. "Not for me thanks. It's only 9 a.m. in Nova Scotia and that's too early, even for me."

"Tea then?" he offered.

"No, I'm fine. Curious, though about being called in. And about where we are sitting."

"Welcome to London." Mullins said. "These offices are fairly new to us, and they are still undergoing some reinforcement and upgrading. We've closed the Churchill War Rooms as a tourist attraction. The official reason is that it doesn't get the tourist traffic it used to, although that's kind of bullshit. Instead, to the public it will be called a research library, but really it's bunker style offices for us. There are six suites on the upper floors, and yours is getting freshened up right now. We felt it necessary to create a hub where our people can work with focus and intensity, though you are welcome to arrange for a place in the countryside for your days off if you want."

"Why here? The agency is created through international cooperation, and agents are from all over the world. Why London?"

Steeves took a sip of Scotch, and said, "It's easy to get anywhere we need to from here, and frankly, the money we need to function comes mostly from European sources. We want you to work with us, and felt that keeping you in Canada meant we'd have to set up a complete satellite bunker and we don't really need to do that given how little work is done there, typically. We could have you work from the US, but I figure'd you might like to be here. You can choose either option once you have a look around."

Mullins continued. "The U.S. administration doesn't want a lot do with us, except when we can bail them out somewhere in Europe. They prefer to have their own agencies handling American things, but the United Kingdom, much of Europe, and the Commonwealth have seen the benefits of what we can do. They want what we offer."

I was still confused about why I was there. "So what exactly is it we are offering?" I said.

"Your...abilities," Steeves said, "would be very helpful to us. And, we'd rather safeguard you here where we can perhaps keep this skill you have secret, and keep you out of harm's way. You are a huge asset Morgan, but I think having the general public know what you can do would be a dangerous thing. The listening you did and intel that you gathered on your last op meant we were able to shut that operation down and none of our people got hurt Morgan. None of them did. Not a single one. We snuck in there, neutralized the bad guys as you call them, and shut down the whole operation."

He was talking about the operation in Sommerside, the one we were in the middle of, when, out of the blue, Jake had his heart attack and died. I bit my bottom lip, and spoke quickly. "You need to know that my abilities have not been working much since Jake died. Although in the last week I have been getting some signs, there's nothing solid. I don't know how much help I will be."

Mullins smiled, "I kind of expected that you might need a warm up. We're happy to provide whatever you need to kickstart things. We're even happy to have you work with us if you can't turn your radar back on. We need you on the team. Tomorrow we can take the chopper up to a shooting range a little way past Peterborough. In the meantime, I can take you on a tour of the situation room. It's where you can safely do most of your work from, if you are able to listen in remotely. I think you'll love the gadgets."

"Alright," I said. "Let's have a look. In the past it helped me to see the locations we were scouting, but when I was peering into that warehouse, I did it all from the boat. If you've got good cameras, it'll help."

We were joined by a woman on our way to the situation room. I looked her up and down carefully. Perfectly styled hair, elegant plaid skirt and a plain black jacket over a silk blouse. Minimal make up. Clipboard.

"I'm Morgan Winfeld," I said, offering my hand to shake. "You must be the psychologist." I stopped myself from saying anything more.

"Yes...well, yes I am... I'm Penny Morrison." In her English accent her last name sounded long and classy, but it didn't hide her nervousness.

"You're tagging along to check me out and make sure I haven't lost my mind during these past six months, right?"

Morrison looked to Steeves and Mullins for some help. She got none as they both stifled laughter.

"Sorry Morgan, I guess we could've warned you that Dr. Marshall would be stopping by." Steeves said.

"I expected it so not to worry, but you could have warned her about me," I said.

"So sorry Ms. Winfeld," she said. "I'm new here and still getting used to it."

"Don't apologize doc. I've known Steeves a long time and he won't steer you wrong. The jury is still out on Director Mullins. Have they let you out into the field yet?"

"No, I'm not a field agent. I'm here as a counsellor and also a profiler."

I looked at Steeves and raised an eyebrow. He knew exactly what I was saying...how on earth would she help anyone if she had no idea of the things we saw, shot at, the people and guns who shot back, and the havoc we encountered by crossing borders, dropping in on people, and blowing shit up?

Steeves smiled, "Now you know why we need you here."

* * *

After a tour of the situation room, which was impressive, I made my way to the tea station in the corner of the large, open space. Dr. Morrison followed me, and stifled a giggle as I searched the area for coffee.

"Tea? There's only tea?" I said. "I can feel my butt dragging and I could really use a coffee."

"There's a coffee shop down the road. We could go and pick one up," she said helpfully.

"Yeah, except getting out of this place and back in would probably take longer than we have. How about Diet Pepsi? See any of that? Is there a fridge? A pop machine?"

"Just tea it seems. And some biscuits if you'd like."

She was nice. I knew we needed to be friends if she was going to get off my case and just let me work, but tea and biscuits was not what I was after.

"Thanks," I said. I returned to where Steeves and Mullins were standing near a large glass top table. I placed my cookies on the edge of it, and watched as Mullins eyes' widened.

"Don't worry Director," I smiled at him. "They are just cookies, and I'm holding this very hot and yet tasteless cup of tea well out of the way."

"You don't have to worry about cookies on here, anyway," said a new voice as I turned around. A thirty-something, fit looking man with bright twinkling blue eyes and a well trimmed beard the colour of dark chocolate approached. He held out his hand, and said, "I'm James. You must be Winfeld. Nice to meet you."

"Good to meet you too," I said. "Is James your first name or last?"

"First. I'm James Callahan."

"Well, if we are going to be on a first named basis, then you'd better call me Morgan."

"Alright," he said. "Want to see how to operate this thing?" He started tapping on the glass top table, moving images around, and then projecting them onto screens that covered a wall. This was the highest tech I had seen in our industry, and it was a thing of beauty to realize just how much we could see and hear from inside a bunker that was pushing 80.

"Winfeld," a voice hailed loudly from the elevator, across the room.

"Stan!" I called back. "It's so good to see you." Stan had helped me out of a jam many times. As the operations manager he was the go to person for field agents. Meeting him felt like seeing an old family friend. He grabbed me in a hug.

"What is it with you guys and the hugs?" I said. "I thought you Brits weren't particularly huggy people. It's something I liked about you."

"Just glad to see you alive, and here," he said, without apology. "We need your help."

"Seems like I should've packed for more than three days."

"Indeed," he said. "Bloody right."

Stan, I soon learned, had started out as a field agent early in his career. He was close to six feet tall, 60ish, and impeccably dressed. He moved like a military man; straight, and with purpose. Nobody who looked at him would know that his left leg was a prosthetic from six inches below his hip. He walked fluidly, spoke directly, and didn't put up with excuses. He was wearing a neatly creased pair of wool pants, and when he removed his overcoat, he was in a black pullover sweater with a crest on the left breast over a shirt and perfectly knotted tie.

I paused.

"What's wrong?" he said, putting his hand on my shoulder. "It looks like you saw a ghost."

"I...you...you've been in my visions in that sweater. But...but you had a trench coat on. But when I described you to Jake, he said that someone in a sweater was sneaking around in Wales...I've seen you in my mind so many times, but I couldn't tell who you were."

"I was in Wales, briefly, when you were there. We needed to scope out that little town you were in and see if there was any risk. Other than meeting a couple of aggressive Rottweilers, everything seemed okay, so I didn't stick around."

"You could've said. My god Stan, those dogs are a pair of sweethearts. I could have introduced you."

"But you're not a dog person," Stan said, smiling.

"No, I'm not. But those dogs are good judges of character apparently." We laughed, and it was good to be there in a room with all these people. My work family. Stan, the protector in my visions and Steeves, both arranging for me to be part of the family again.

James started bringing up new screens. I recognized the faces of agents I had met in the past, and a series of maps. It was going to get interesting.

Steeves spoke. "Your role Morgan, if you're willing, will be as a senior point of contact for our agents in the field. You'll work closely with Stan, sending intel back and forth to them to keep them safe. We are not telling them how you know things – it would probably just freak them out, and, we need to protect that talent of yours."

Mullins continued.   "We've got some issues in eastern Europe that need dealing with, and we have field agents going in, but they're going to need some help. We want you to work here, from head office, and be their front line."

I felt like I was repeating myself, but I had to tell them, "Guys, I hate to tell you this again, but the visions have been gone for six months. I mean, I've had a little activity recently, a few dreams, but it's like a switch turned off in there. And remember, when it did work I was out in the field where I was in the middle of things."

"Doesn't matter if you don't get your skills back really. We've got a lot of new people, first time in the field for us. They are pretty wet behind the ears and need some mentoring. Hopefully you can stretch your reach if we've got the right technology set up, and if not, you'll be an ideal resource. We want to make sure that you are physically safe, plus as you've said before, it's getting way too hard to move people in and out of other countries." Stan said. "Right now, we've got field agents hiding out in little villages and towns scattered all over the place. We don't have time to waste."

After that meeting, I made a call to my cousin Helen in Wales. I told her I needed some emergency tutoring. So it seems like I am back to work and I can set my journal aside. There will be no time for writing in the foreseeable future.

PART THREE

CHAPTER 35

Morgan called Helen again the next morning and left another message before heading to work.

"Stan," she said, entering the central room, "I haven't heard from Helen, but I'm ready to start leveraging the technical equipment and see what I can learn."

"Good," he said. "Let's get to work. We have two agents in Budapest..."

Morgan sat on a tall stool in front of the glass top table. "James," she said quietly. "I'm going to need some help."

James came and stood beside her, a mug of coffee in his hand. "Okay, let's see what you've got Morgan."

"Hang on," she said. "I think I need some of that coffee you are drinking."

"Oh this," he said. "I don't drink coffee. This is for you."

"We are going to get along just fine," she said, smiling for the first time that day.

"I have it on good authority we will," he smiled back. He was in his late twenties, tall, slender, with long arms and legs. His goatee didn't quite hide dimples, and his brown eyes danced with laughter as he handed her the coffee.

James tapped on the table top, and projected a video screen onto the wall. A satellite map came up on the table.

"I heard you need to see as much as possible. So here I've got satellite images from the last 48 hours of the location in Budapest. The people around there are probably speaking a couple of different languages. If I could pick up signals that were loud enough I could run the dialogue through a translator, but we aren't getting any sound at all."

"Makes sense," Morgan said. "Budapest is an old place, with thick walls in their historic buildings, just like we have here."

"Yes, that's true, though these buildings are newer. If we could get someone on the inside to place a few bugs this would be easier..."

"Yeah, I know it seems easier. But getting into places and planting listening devices is almost impossible now. There is so much security everywhere that even the most cunning of covert operatives cannot get in there without getting caught," Morgan said, thinking of the last time she was in Ukraine with Jake. She shook her head to clear it. "James can you zoom in any closer? These images are not that clear."

"I can, but the resolution starts to go and then they get even fuzzier."

Morgan chewed her lip for a moment. "What about using Google Maps? They have street views and everything. It might give me a better sense of the place."

"Give me a moment, and I'll bring them in through a secure portal so we can't be tracked." James said. He returned to his computer terminal a few feet away and got to work.

Morgan looked at the room closely. This was nothing like covert operations she'd "grown up" with as a field agent. She suddenly yearned for a field exercise, racing across snow on a snowmobile, or down the highway in the fastest car possible. She sipped her coffee and waited impatiently.

"Okay," James finally said. "Have a look at the left screen, and there's the street on Google Maps. There's a café next door to our target, and that building there," he pointed with a glowing dot on the screen, "is where we think they are. Our satellite photos show a lot of action on that building. They are travelling in business style sedan cars. You'll see photos of the guys we are looking for, here on the tabletop screen."

Morgan poured herself into the work, evaluating images, looking at people's faces. James went quiet as he watched from a distance. He was very curious to see if the talk about Morgan was true. Could she really see and hear things when there was nothing for her to hear and little to see?

Morgan hopped off her stool abruptly. "I need to go for a walk," she announced as she left the room.

She headed out through security and the quiet of the bunker, and walked down the street. She looked like any other tourist in London with her jeans and t-shirt, until someone looked closer. The fine lines around her eyes that told a story of someone who'd had some life experience. There was noticeable grey shooting through her dark brown hair. And unlike other tourists, she was without an umbrella, despite the pouring rain.

Morgan walked quickly, dodging around people on the sidewalk, and twice she walked in the gutter to avoid being poked by open umbrellas.

Get it together Winfeld, she sternly thought to herself. She knew that Helen could tap into some perceptions at a distance. It was how Helen knew Morgan was looking for her, and it was how she figured out that Morgan was in the spy business.

How do you do it Helen, Morgan asked. *And where the hell are you?*

She turned a corner and caught movement out of the corner of her eye. People were going into a café to escape the weather and grab a hot drink. *Too bad I didn't grab my wallet*, she thought. *This is probably where James got that coffee from.* She tucked her hands into the pockets of her jacket, and bent her head into the rain. She looked for a quiet doorway and stopped in it, out of the rain but within view of the café. She watched a couple enter. *Lean in*, she told herself. *Who are they? What're they saying?* After a moment, she could hear the sound of water rushing in her ears. Then, the scraping of a chair on the floor, and someone settling down to sit at a table. She squinted her eyes half shut, and then moving through a cloud, it was as though she was standing in the café. She saw a woman wiggling to get out of her wet raincoat.

Okay, this is something at least. The radar's back on. Now I just need it with details. In her mind, unbidden, came a vision of Helen's parlour. Her dogs nearby, a fire in the grate. And then suddenly, Helen. Morgan shook herself away from the vision, grabbed her cell and dialed Helen's number.

"Hi Morgan, I got your messages. Sorry for the delay, I was on a little holiday with my kids. You okay?"

"Well, whatever okay is, I could be okay but honestly, I'm frustrated. I'm trying to peek into stuff that's happening far away and I'm having issues."

"You're back at work, though. That's good. You needed something to do. How can I help?"

"Helen, I need to be able to use this listening stuff at much greater distances. I need to apply it to see inside of places that I can't get into." Morgan was careful not to say too much, in case someone was monitoring their call.

"I think you've got a big wish there, Morgan. Although you can learn to sense things at a distance, actually dialling into conversations, well, you're asking for something that barely works when you're next door to someone. It's like me tapping in to what you are up to when you are far away. I can get glimpses, but it's not like having a hidden microphone."

Morgan carefully told Helen about listening from the boat, on her last assignment with Jake. She could hear the sleeping bad guys as they snored, listen in on their conversations, plus she picked up a detailed layout of everything inside the warehouse.

"You could see the lights? You could hear snoring?"

"Yes."

"Well, Morgan, you're already better at this than you think. If I could do what you do, I wouldn't have to visit my kids to know how they are. Your confidence is just a little shattered. Think back...exactly what were you doing when you got all that detail?"

Morgan closed her eyes as the rain came harder into her doorway. "I was sitting in the dark on the deck of a boat, sipping Scotch to stay warm...and leaning in really hard. But I don't know what tipped me over the edge to where I could see all of that."

"Morgan, you just need to give yourself permission to practice until you get the hang of it again. Try and recreate the exact circumstances, no matter what it is. Start with something close to you, and slowly increase the distance. Try it without the drink."

Morgan left the café and headed back toward the bunker. She could practice this skill, and just like learning to be a crack shot, she would get better at it. She placed her feet one in front of the other on the old cobblestones, her ankles turning slightly with the uneven surface. *The pavement is a metaphor,* she thought. *The individual stones could be uneven, bumpy, broken and cracked, but taken together they all lead to the same place.* She hadn't been born a spy, but she learned to be good at it. Being an empath or reader or whatever it was she was doing would be the same.

As she approached the Churchill Research Library, and the covert operations inside, she saw a familiar face. James was waiting near the reception area as she entered, and he escorted her through security and then walked with her back to the operations centre.

"How's all this sitting with you?" he asked.

"It's pretty weird to be honest. I really need to get my skills back if I'm going to be any help at all."

"My mum called and told me to give you whatever you need, and I just want to let you know I am here for you. We all are."

"Your mum?"

"Helen Davies."

"Helen Davies?"

"My work name is James Callahan."

James explained that he was in training to become the new Stan, since Stan had to retire eventually. Stan was teaching James everything he could about protecting field agents. James was applying what he learned, along with his degrees in computer science and cybersecurity. He'd completed training as a field agent the previous summer, and although he found it wasn't quite his thing, he knew that it was already helping him to be a better analyst. He was hoping to go on a few more exercises this winter to keep up his training, and also test some new equipment.

"How did you get this job?"

"Stan recruited me. It was around the same time you were doing some work with my mum. They know I don't have the powers you do – my mum and siblings seemed to get all of that – but they seem to like what I've done so far."

"You're Helen's son." Morgan blinked as she adjusted to the information.

"I am," he smiled.

"How'd you like to come to Bangor, Maine with me and celebrate American Thanksgiving? I'll introduce you to some more cousins."

"Maine? In America?"

"Yes, that one. Of course."

"Are these real cousins, or the kind of people my mother calls cousins?"

"These are distant cousins, but they are real ones. And they cook up some pretty good food."

"Plus it will be somewhere you can work on eavesdropping?"

"Yes, exactly. Everyone thinks I'm retired from work as a human resources manager. It's something safe and boring enough no one asks about it."

"Aren't you kind of young to be retired?"

"Yes, though my boring back story means I can do whatever I need to, plus I have a habit of getting people to talk about themselves so I don't have to. Now, let's head back to the centre and get these folks sorted out in Budapest."

CHAPTER 36

"Commander Steeves, you wanted to see me?" Morgan presented herself at the office early the next morning. Director Mullins joined them.

"Yes, I understand you are flying out to Maine for American Thanksgiving? And taking young Callahan with you?"

"I am. We'll visit, eat turkey, and maybe do some shopping. Is there something else you need me to do while I am there?"

"Yes, I'd like you to make two stops, one in Virginia and one in Washington. These will be a brief meet and greet, to introduce you."

"Isn't CIA headquarters in Virginia, and FBI in Washington? I thought the Americans didn't want to work with us?"

"They don't officially, but I like to keep my options open, and fostering these relationships is important. You can introduce yourself as Assistant Director of Field Operations. Congratulations."

"Sir?"

"You're not a field agent anymore, Winfeld. We need you pulling our folks out of trouble and gathering intelligence like you did for the people we just extracted from Budapest."

Mullins smiled, and offered his hand for a congratulatory handshake. "Let me be the second one to congratulate you."

"Um...how are we going to explain what I do? If I'm not in the field gathering intel, making me an assistant director of field operations sounds like I have the wrong label."

"We're positioning you as someone who is actively involved in all field operations, but from our headquarters here instead of being deployed. I want our colleagues at the FBI and CIA to know that we have increased our capacity, though they will probably assume it is through the use of technological tools," Steeves said.

"Alright, I can do that. Do I need to do anything different? Wear something special? Don't the American feds wear dark suits and ties?"

"Yeah, but you're not them. You could spring for a few new t-shirts, and maybe get a haircut, but I think your leather jacket and jeans uniform nicely conveys our badass attitude for getting things done."

"With this promotion, I assume that Callahan and I will be flying first class?"

"Fat chance, Winfeld." Mullins laughed.

"Sir, with respect, most of the managers I know travel first class with their assistants once they make it big. I only want the same for myself. Besides, this is no longer a quick trip for Thanksgiving, it's now a business trip." She looked at both men, her eyes dark and clear. She crossed her arms across her chest, and stood with one booted foot slightly ahead of the other. Mullins caved in first, and Steeves laughed.

"Alright," Mullins said, "but I encourage you not to keep up with this demanding stuff."

"Sir, it's not just me. Think about Callahan and trying to squeeze his long legs into economy class seats."

"Field operatives don't typically fly first class."

"No, but then you've just said I'm not a field operative. I'm an assistant director, travelling with the cybersecurity officer of an international agency that no one wants to admit is necessary."

"Fine," Mullins said. "You've made your point. I expect I'll get flack when the expense reports are released to the member countries."

"Then maybe it's time they started committing some people to these ops," Morgan said.

CHAPTER 37

"Oh my gawd, you actually made it! I was worried you were just teasing me and you were going to cancel!" Colette said at the airport.

"Why would I do that," Morgan laughed as she prepared herself for her cousin's embrace. "You know I wanted to see you."

"Maybe because you cancelled last year, and a couple of years before that!" Colette laughed. "You remember Brian, my better half?"

"I'd like you to meet one of our cousins from across the pond. This is James, and he's confirmed that he is a second cousin four times removed from you."

"My gawd, people actually figure that stuff out," Brian said, clapping James on the shoulder.

"We've got a crowd of 18 for dinner tomorrow, and still some prep to do when we get to the farm. Are you up for peeling stuff?"

"Sure, whatever you need," Morgan said, rolling her eyes at James.

"I'm pretty good with setting the table," James offered.

"How do you feel about stuffing the turkeys," Brian asked. "I always end up with that job and can't stand it. I think in another life I was a vegetarian."

"Don't be such a chicken," Colette said, throwing her head back to laugh. "Get it...chicken...but we're stuffing a turkey."

As they put their carry on luggage in the truck, Colette whispered to Morgan, "Is the book in there? I get to read it, right? Tell me you brought it!"

"Book?" said James.

"No, I'm still working on it," Morgan said. "Remember I told you the publisher wanted some more spit and polish to the manuscript?"

"That you did, and you said she gave you two weeks," Colette turned in the car to look at Morgan.

"I sent it to her," Morgan confirmed.

"You wrote a book?" James asked again.

"It's about work," Morgan said looking at him. "So it's kind of hard to write."

"But you said there was some adventure to it, and even a bit of romance. I want to read it so bad," Colette said. "I want to see some excitement about working in HR. Especially if there's some mystery, intrigue, and some romance involved."

* * *

THANK YOU

I spent six years in the Canadian Armed Forces, then went on to work as a teacher, career counsellor, writer, and instructional designer. Having a variety of jobs, and having lived across the country, I try to draw from those experiences and the amazing people I've met to give depth to my writing. I enjoy turning random thoughts and unnerving dreams into stories, and it was a couple of dreams plus some historical research that led me to create Morgan Winfeld's world.

My work has been published in collections of short stories, magazines, an earlier novel, and some ghost writing. The first assignment to get me excited about writing came from my sixth grade teacher, Mr. Burrows. He asked me to ghostwrite a story that started me down a path of researching, reading, and eventually gathering an admirable collection of rejection emails.

This novella is the first story about Morgan Winfeld. If you'd like to learn what's coming up next, I hope you'll keep in touch, and connect online. If you've enjoyed the book, please leave a review on Amazon, Goodreads, Indigo, or wherever you like to find reviews that encourage you to read a new book. Reviews really help people to find my stories, and encourage me to keep writing new ones for you!

Facebook PamRWriter   Instagram @PamDRobertson
Twitter @PamRobertson   Web pamrobertson.org

Join the newsletter for information on upcoming books, free stories, and more (without getting spammed of course!)
bit.ly/pamsnewsletter

Printed in Great
Britain
by Amazon